Because of You

a Blue Harbor novel

OLIVIA MILES

Rosewood Press

ALSO BY OLIVIA MILES

Blue Harbor Series
A Place for Us
Second Chance Summer

Stand-Alone Titles
Meet Me at Sunset
This Christmas

Oyster Bay Series
Feels Like Home
Along Came You
Maybe This Time
This Thing Called Love
Those Summer Nights
Christmas at the Cottage
Still the One
One Fine Day
Had to Be You

Misty Point Series
One Week to the Wedding
The Winter Wedding Plan

Sweeter in the City Series
Sweeter in the Summer
Sweeter Than Sunshine
No Sweeter Love
One Sweet Christmas

Briar Creek Series
Mistletoe on Main Street
A Match Made on Main Street
Hope Springs on Main Street
Love Blooms on Main Street
Christmas Comes to Main Street

Harlequin Special Edition
'Twas the Week Before Christmas
Recipe for Romance

Because of You

Fall was in the air and already the leaves on the maple trees that lined Main Street were tipped with orange, falling softly in the breeze as they made their way gently to the pavement. Maddie Conway resisted the urge to gather a few like she had as a child. Usually, she loved Blue Harbor at this time of year—it brought up memories of back to school shopping and cozy new soft wool sweaters (even if they were often passed down by her three older sisters), and coming home to their big, lakefront Victorian, walking into the warm kitchen, and seeing her mother at the big center island, inviting her to help with an apple or pumpkin pie.

But this afternoon, as Maddie walked home from the family orchard to the smaller house she shared with her sister Amelia, she couldn't help but feel a nervous flutter. And no matter how much she tried to quicken her pace or tell herself that it would all be okay, she just couldn't quite convince herself. She'd even walked—all the way from Conway Orchard—when she could have easily accepted a ride from her eldest sister Britt, who more often than not gave her a ride there and back each week, so the pies Maddie baked at home and sold at the market wouldn't get damaged. She'd thought the fresh air would do her some good, that the exercise would work out the anxiety. She'd taken her sweet time. Detoured—by a couple of hours, she now realized. Delayed the inevitable return to her apartment with her spreadsheets and lists. Told herself that she would clear her head first.

So much for that.

It was Sunday, and in their family, Sunday was reserved for two things: market day and family dinner, at least it had once…Still, this evening they would be reinstating that tradition, even if it wasn't going to be a weekly thing now that all four sisters had flown the nest and their father…Well, their father had finally moved on, more than fourteen years after the loss of his wife. Something all the sisters tried to tell each other was a good thing, even if their eyes didn't lie. It was an adjustment period. For all of them, Maddie reminded herself, knowing that she wasn't alone and never had been. She had three sisters, a loving father, cousins, friends…she was surrounded by support in her hometown. But some days, it just didn't feel that way.

Maddie had spent the morning selling her homemade pies at Conway Orchard like she did every week. The orchard and winery that had been in her family for generations; it was something she was proud to be part of, something that had allowed her to hone her skills, something that cemented her place in her beloved Michigan town. She'd set one pie aside for tonight's dinner, knowing that if she brought it to the market, it would be snatched up without her even noticing until it was too late, and she intended to stop by home, grab it, and go. The longer she lingered, the more she would fret. And pace. And think that really, she should have used the day doing something at the storefront that would soon be her bakery rather than bake pies for the market, because, at this rate, she'd never get her business open. And then winter would hit. And winter in Blue Harbor was cold. So cold that even the locals didn't get out as much. And really, she should have thought about all that before she decided to use all of her savings to take the vacant spot next to her sister's café, and quit her steady job there, too.

Maybe, Amelia would take her back. She chewed her lip, wondering if this was possible. Maybe, her sister would even want to expand and buy her out. Firefly Café was one of the most popular destinations in town, and seating for the outdoor patio was always in high demand on the warmer evenings. Maybe, Maddie could just pretend that brief moment of insanity when she declared she would start her own bakery could all be forgotten. Life could go back to normal. It would be comfortable and safe.

She'd feel things out with Amelia tonight, at dinner.

With her anxiety under control for the moment at least, Maddie let herself into the garden unit of the house owned by her sister and grabbed her pie from where it was cooling on the counter in her small kitchen. Apple, of course. She only used what was in season, and right now the orchard was bursting with apples of different colors and sizes, and tourists who came to enjoy one last getaway weekend in the quaint, lakeside town that she had called home all her life, but never took for granted.

Yes, she told herself again, it would be all right. She

loved where she lived, and she loved what she did, and she had the unwavering support of her family at her side.

She just didn't want to let them down.

With her pie in hand, she locked her door, walked up the stairs to Amelia's front door, and knocked, only to remember that since the café closed early on Sundays, Amelia was helping Britt with a wine tasting at the orchard this afternoon. Britt had mentioned they would arrive at the house together, but by then Maddie had sold out of pies and had no excuse to linger and was no longer distracted by all the lively conversation with familiar faces at the market, and her mind was wandering, back to scary territory. Back to her long, chaotic list of things big and small that would all need to be accounted for if she actually planned to go through with opening her bakery.

By house, Britt meant their childhood home that was tucked at the base of a tree-lined street, its back to Lake Huron, where the girls would splash and swim all summer long. Maddie opted to walk, knowing that the more she kept busy, the less the nerves could get to her. She held the pie in both hands, knowing that if she dropped it, Britt would be mighty disappointed, and so would their father. The man had always loved a good pie, especially with the fruit from his own crops.

But the pie was delivered safely, the walk passed by in a blur, and Maddie was happy to see that she wasn't the first of her sisters to arrive. Cora was helping their father shuck the last of the summer corn on the front porch as she approached.

"Oh good," Dennis said, grinning at her. "Now I can pass the reins."

She smiled. He knew she'd always enjoyed this task as a girl, more than Cora at least, who looked bored as she set another ear of corn in a basket.

"Trade you then," Maddie said, handing her father the pie box.

He took in the smell, smiling at what he'd determined. "Apple. It's officially fall."

"Not quite," Maddie said. Fall was still a week away, technically speaking. Still, it was close enough.

"Well, I for one am ready for the change of season," Cora said when their father disappeared through the front door with the dessert, letting the screen door slap shut behind him.

"Easy for you to say," Maddie commented. "You own a holiday shop!"

"True," Cora said ruefully. "But I still see most of my sales during tourist season. It's always nice when things quiet down and the town becomes our own again, though."

Maddie settled onto a wicker chair and pulled an ear of corn from the basket. "True."

"You don't sound so sure of that," Cora remarked. She frowned as she brushed at the corn silks on her lap.

Maddie wasn't sure of anything lately. She had planned to get her bakery open by October, but now that date was starting to feel a little optimistic. Amelia's boyfriend, Matt Bradford, had drawn up the plans for the renovation of the space, and, seeing as he was on the town zoning commission in addition to being an architect, he'd pushed through the plans for the permit, too. She was all ready to start construction and turn what had once been a stationery store into the bakery of her dreams; only now that it was no longer a dream, but a pressing, all-consuming reality, she felt overwhelmed with decisions, and details, and things that were not part of her wheelhouse.

She knew flour and sugar and butter. She could make a perfect pie crust with her eyes closed, but when it came to things like pricing and furniture and overhead and budget, she felt downright queasy.

Before she had a chance to respond to Cora, Britt's car pulled up onto the gravel driveway, and their two older sisters hopped out of the car. As usual, Britt brought with her wine and cider from the orchard, and Amelia had leftovers from today's wine pairings.

"Couldn't let this brie go to waste," she said, revealing an entire wheel that hadn't been sliced.

Maddie's stomach growled in anticipation. She'd been too busy looking at light fixture options on her laptop to grab breakfast before the market, and then too busy at the market to stop to eat.

"What was the event today?" Cora asked. It was a new offering at the family business; one of Britt's many ambitions to grow the orchard and vineyard and give them a cushion for the leaner, winter months. "Another bachelorette party?"

"Sixtieth birthday," Britt said with a little smile. "But it may as well have been a bachelorette party. These women were wild!"

Maddie laughed. "I hope we're still able to have fun when we're that age."

"I don't see why not!" Amelia remarked, but Maddie wasn't so convinced. Things were changing, and quickly. Britt and Amelia were both reunited with their high school sweethearts now, and it didn't take a genius to know what that meant. They were soul mates, first loves, picking up right where they'd left off, and happily so. There was none of the worry about when to call, when the next date would be, or if things would last.

No doubt one of them would be engaged by spring, the other by summer. And then...then everything would change.

Maddie finished shucking the last of her corn. "I wonder what's on the menu tonight," she said, meeting Amelia's eye.

She saw her other sisters glance at each other, too. Since their father had started seeing Candy, she had introduced a new cuisine into their lives. Gone were the traditional meals they had come to expect with Sunday night dinners of the past when their mother would make a tray of lasagna or a roasted turkey, or, when the weather was still warm enough to eat outside, grilled fish and corn, which Maddie might have thought they were having tonight, but knew from recent experience would not be the case.

"Should we take bets?" Amelia asked, giving her a wink.

"Ha," Maddie said, but she might have done if she wasn't pinching every penny with the start up of her new business.

Really, she told herself, as she followed her sisters

through the door, she should feel comforted by the fact that she had grown up in a family business, and that each of her sisters now owned or operated their own business too.

But instead of feeling prepared, she felt overwhelmed. And maybe even a little threatened.

The house was quiet as they walked down the hallway, past the rows of family photos that still hung on the walls, mercifully unchanged, and past the dining room, which was not set with placemats or glasses, or any indication that dinner would be taking place. Maddie idly wondered if this was going to be a family dinner like a couple of weeks back when Candy announced they'd all be eating on TV trays because the season finale of one of her favorite dating shows was on, and Amelia had barely been able to contain her glee because she was a closet viewer of that show too—something Maddie only knew because she lived below her and the walls were thin.

Still, it was a bit worrisome. Candy was different than their mother in every possible way, and despite all the sisters feeling apprehensive about their father finding someone new after fourteen years, Candy didn't seem to be going anywhere, and they were all learning to adjust. Some sooner than others.

"Oh! They're here!" a voice trilled from the open screen door at the back of the house, and before Maddie had time to prepare herself, Candy burst into the kitchen, her arms open wide, her smile big, and her eyes downright eager.

Maddie went to scoot behind Cora, but she wasn't

quick enough, and before she knew it, she was Candy's first victim—make that only victim, because her sisters used the opportunity to dash out to the back porch. Traitors.

Candy's arms pulled her close to her sizable bosom and kept her there as Candy swayed jauntily from side to side. Even with her face muffled into Candy's shoulder, Maddie could hear the smile in the woman's voice when she said, "I've been looking forward to this all day!"

The hug or the dinner? Probably both.

A wave of shame came down over Maddie as Candy released her. She was trying, and her intentions were in the right place. And she made their father so happy. Happier than Maddie could remember seeing him since she was just a kid, really, and sadly, those memories were a bit fuzzy.

"I made something *really* special for tonight!" Candy bit her lip and rubbed her hands together eagerly, and, with knowing dread, Maddie followed her out onto the back porch where, to her horror, a pig was roasting on a spit.

For a moment, she thought she might pass out. Or scream.

Candy must have seen the reaction in her face, because she said, "You're not a vegetarian, all of a sudden, are you?"

She was not, but today…Today she was.

With a tight smile, she averted her eyes and walked quickly toward her father, who was standing at the grill. Maddie was almost afraid to ask what was inside, but

9

when he caught her expression, he winked at her and said, "Burgers. Just in case."

"Dad." Maddie's voice was thick with emotion. Surely he remembered the time that she had been asked to dissect a baby pig in biology class, and had instead hidden in the bathroom, with tears streaming down her face, to the endless delight of the boys in her grade. She'd never eaten bacon again. Didn't bake with it either, which was a shame, really.

He just gave her a kind smile and said, "She's trying. Just…give her a chance."

Maddie pulled in a breath and went to join her sisters, who were huddled around the picnic table, which today bore a festive cloth that Candy must have put out for the occasion. Even if it was pink. Like pigs, Maddie couldn't help but think with a small whimper. But it was Candy's unabashed favorite color and that was more likely the reason behind it.

She sat with her back to the massacre going on behind her. She felt tears prickle her eyes.

It was Amelia who set a hand on hers, looking downright amused. She knew all about the biology class incident. Their mother was gone by then, and Britt was in college, and Amelia had been the one to write a note to the teacher, begging for an alternative assignment and citing emotional distress as the cause.

"Dad ambushed us the moment we walked outside, so we had some preparation. I know it was a shock, but I guess it's something that Candy's family did once a year, at special cookouts."

"You did always love ham and cheese sandwiches when you were little," Britt said gently. She started to sputter on a laugh, and Amelia elbowed her when Maddie narrowed her eyes.

"It's just...too much."

"Everything about Candy is too much," Cora sighed. "But that's just how she is."

"You know how I felt when I first met her. Seeing her here, in the house, doting on Dad the way she did." Now it was Britt's turn to narrow her eyes. "But she's a good person. And Dad's happy. And we shouldn't expect him to be alone forever, especially now that we've all left the house."

Maddie grumbled in response. "I guess it could be worse. You're the one who has her working for you now," she said to Amelia.

Maddie wondered now if part of her impatience with Candy was because the woman had essentially replaced her at Amelia's café. It was a job she had held for years, and loved, not just because she got to work side by side with her sister but because she got to bake. And because, truth be told, she felt safe. Amelia always took care of her.

When Maddie had decided to take over the empty space beside Firefly Café for her own bakery, Amelia had hired (or willingly allowed) Candy to help out on a few shifts. And that meant there was no going back. Maddie had put her plan into action. Her wonderful, secure spot at the café was no longer hers at all.

"Remember how we used to have tea parties out here for Mother's Day?" she said wistfully. Sometimes it was

11

so much better to look back on the good times, to remember how it used to be before everything changed.

Cora gave a little smile. "Mom would bring out all the
fancy china. You loved the patterns of birds and flowers."

Maddie hadn't thought about those dishes in years, but
Cora was right. She did love them. They were no doubt
still in the cabinet in the dining room, tucked away.
"None of them really matched," she said, thinking of it
now. "I think half of the fun of it was seeing which cup
and saucer we would end up with each year."

"Mom made everything beautiful," Britt said, and they
all agreed. Each of them had kept a small part of her alive
in them. It was why Maddie still made the pies. Why she
was here, for Sunday night dinner, even though it was
nothing like it should have been.

She felt a solid hand on her shoulder and she looked
up to see their father leaning over them. "I'll take care of
the…situation. Away from the table. Let's just try to have
a good time tonight." Dennis gave a tight smile.

When Maddie saw the plea in his eyes, she nodded.
She could do that.

"This will help," Britt said, uncorking one of the wine
bottles. It was the newest blend, named for her boyfriend's daughter, Keira, a sweet little girl whom Maddie
knew would be her first and most loyal patron once the
bakery opened. She loved the cookies that Maddie used to
make for the café.

Just thinking of that gave her the courage she needed,
and for a moment, at least, the nerves were replaced by
something closer to excitement. Maybe she'd make a dif-

ferent cookie each week. And something special for the holidays. A boxed gift set? The possibilities were endless. Sometimes that was thrilling. Sometimes it was just confusing.

They sipped their wine as Candy and "Denny," as Candy liked to call him, finished up the meal preparations. The bite in the air was just enough to offset the waning of the warm sun, and Maddie pulled up her turtleneck closer to her chin, enjoying the way the red wine warmed her throat.

As promised, Denny made sure that all the food was brought to the table in appropriate presentations, and Maddie helped herself to an ear of corn as Candy lit some citronella candles. She had really thought of everything, right down to the little corn cob holders in the shape of…little pigs.

Maddie closed her eyes, briefly.

"So Britt, how are things at the orchard? Harvest Fest is coming up soon!" Candy asked eagerly and sipped her wine, no doubt waiting for her chance to offer her services.

"Just around the corner," Britt said, nodding. "Robbie and I are planning on making this year's festival better than ever." Her smile dropped as she glanced at her father. "No offense meant, Dad."

"None taken," he said good-naturedly. "You're doing exactly what I'd hoped you'd do when you took over the business. You're making it your own, but upholding our traditions. I couldn't be more proud."

Britt beamed, and Maddie couldn't help but feel a stir

of unease shift inside her. She took another bite of her corn, not caring that some got stuck in her teeth. It wasn't like she'd be kissing anyone later tonight. She didn't even have time for a pet fish these days.

"And how is that handsome man of yours?" Candy continued, waggling her eyebrows at Britt. "I haven't seen Robbie much recently, but then, I've been so busy at the café lately."

"Business will wind down by the time the leaves have all fallen," Amelia said.

Candy looked a bit ruffled. "Well, now that you're co-zy with that adorable Matt Bradford again, you know I'm happy to help whenever you need me."

Amelia nodded politely. Amelia was good at that.

"And now what about you girls?" Candy turned her attention on Cora and Maddie. Cora's eyes were wide, and Maddie didn't need to say anything to know that her sister was thinking the exact same thing that she was—there was no getting out of this. When Candy wanted something, she got it. And tonight, it would seem she had chosen to turn her attention to their love lives, or, in Maddie and Cora's case, lack thereof.

"Just busy at the shop," Cora said casually. "More and more people are starting to think of the holidays now, and I'm planning my window themes."

Candy didn't look interested in window themes or Christmas conversation. She looked at Maddie, who wasn't able to shift her gaze quick enough. "And you, Maddie? Anyone special in your life?"

Maddie shook her head. "I'm really swamped trying to

get my bakery open." She gave a little smile as if that were that. Really, she wasn't sure which was worse—talking about her bakery or her love life. Both felt so uncertain.

But Candy said, "Well, I'm happy to help! You know, what Cora just said had me thinking about themes. Have you thought about a theme for your bakery? People love those. I know I do." She picked up her paper napkin, and it was only then that Maddie noticed the sweet little pig face printed on it.

Maddie didn't need a theme for her bakery, at least not one in Candy's sense of the word. "The building permit just came in and I need to find a contractor, so..." She gave a little wince, hoping that Candy would take her hint.

"You planning to use Gus?" her dad asked.

Maddie nodded. "I put a call into him already, but haven't heard back." Actually, she'd put in three calls. He'd left a message after the first, and she hadn't been able to get in touch with him again.

She took a big gulp of wine, fighting back the worry in her stomach.

Candy's eyes were gleaming with interest. "Who is this Gus fellow?"

Amelia laughed. "Don't get any ideas, Candy. He's about seventy, but he's the best in town."

"Unless you want to use Cole," Cora said, raising her eyebrows. She explained to Candy, "Cole does handiwork, too, but he's...weird. Keeps to himself. Always did, even back in school. He still lives just up the street, at his mother's house. We used to see him at the bus stop each morning."

Maddie picked at her corn. She hadn't thought about those days in a long time. Hadn't heard the name Cole McCarthy in a long time, either. He rarely came into town, and when he was ever at the pub at the Carriage House Inn, Maddie's hangout of choice, he sat at the bar, shoulders hunched, talked to no one, and left without a glance around the room. He was an odd kid who'd grown into an odd man. Unsettling, if anyone were to ask her.

"He keeps to himself mostly," Amelia commented. "But he's a big guy. He's fixed up his mother's house quite a bit over the years."

Candy nodded slowly. "I see." She squinted her eyes, taking a thoughtful sip of her wine. "Tell you what, Maddie," she said, sitting a little straighter as her smile took over her face. "What don't you let me get that contractor lined up for you? You know how hard it can be to track these guys down, and it will be one less thing for you to worry about."

Maddie opened her mouth to decline the offer, but one glance at her father told her to reconsider. She did have a lot of work to do. More than she could handle, really. And Candy was persuasive by nature. Maybe she could get Gus to return her calls and commit to the project.

"Thanks, Candy," she said, and Candy beamed as she clasped her hands together and dug back into her plate of food.

Maddie exchanged a look of camaraderie with Amelia as she reached for her wine glass. Really, that hadn't been so bad. So Candy wanted to help, and Maddie supposed that there was no harm in letting her.

2

Cole McCarthy loaded his toolbox into the back of his truck and hesitated for a moment, looking back at the front door of his childhood home—his only home— fighting the urge to go back inside the house for one more check on his mother, but he knew she'd just shoo him away, and even though that was meant to reassure him, it never worked.

He squinted into the sun as he looked up at the house, taking in the row of three windows on the second floor, and the roof that he had patched last fall. The yellow paint was chipping and could use a fresh coat. He'd pick up some paint in town, tackle the project before the weather turned and it became too cold for outdoor projects. It would be a surprise for his mother. Might even put a smile on her face.

And it was something he could do. Something within his control. Because nothing else was, it seemed. Never had been.

He closed his eyes briefly and opened the driver-side door, his eye catching on some movement behind the big hydrangea bush that bore his mother's favorite flowers during the summertime. His attention now caught, he turned, watching as a woman came into view. Her smile was large, her wave animated, and he wondered if she knew him somehow, or just thought she did.

He would certainly have remembered her. Big, blonde hair in perky curls, and a bright pink dress that showed every curve. She was wearing heels, and she seemed to struggle for balance as she maneuvered her way along the gravel drive. No coat, but then it was a warm day for September. Might even be the last of it.

He raised a hand and hoped she would keep going, be on her way, but her blue eyes had an eager glint that told him even though he might not recognize her, she knew exactly where she was.

The question then, was why?

Cole leaned a hip against his truck. "Can I help you?"

"I was just out for a walk…" the woman started, but she hesitated when she saw Cole drop his gaze to her extremely impractical shoes. Her smile turned a little guilty when he met her eye. "Well, I happened to see you loading that toolbox into the back of your truck, and I wondered…are you…do you…"

"I'm a contractor," Cole finished for her. "Handyman." Jack of all trades. However you wanted to spin it.

"Then it looks like I'm in exactly the right place at the right time!"

He narrowed his eyes on her, fighting off a grin. "That so?" Wasn't that convenient? For a moment he wondered if his mother or her equally nosey friend Janice had arranged this. There was no telling what those two really discussed over a cup of tea, but if it made his mother laugh, he couldn't argue with it, even if he suspected they were hatching a way to find him a love life. But this woman was too old for him. Surely this couldn't have been their doing.

"I'm Candace. Candace Conway? Well, not really, not officially, but it has a nice ring to it, doesn't it?" She gave a loud laugh. "And I pretty much live right down the road, at the Conway home? But everyone calls me Candy," the woman said, extending a hand that revealed bright pink nail polish.

"Cole McCarthy," he said, giving it a shake. "Don't think I've seen you before."

"I'm from Pine Falls, originally," Candy said, referring to the neighboring town.

Ah. Cole slammed his trunk closed. Explained why she was talking to him then. "What can I do for you?"

"Well, it's not for me, actually," Candy said hurriedly. "It's for my boyfriend's daughter. She's starting a bakery, you see, and she just mentioned to me the other night that she was looking for a contractor."

"Seems like a big project," Cole remarked. He didn't get many of those. Usually, the work he handled consisted of minor household chores that people either didn't trust themselves with or didn't have time for, not that he was complaining. He lifted his chin, curious. "I didn't know a bakery was opening."

"Next to Firefly Café," Candy explained. "Maddie Conway. *Beautiful* girl. Right around your age, I think. Maybe a couple of years younger. You must know her…?"

If he didn't know better, he might think this Candy

woman was batting her eyes at him. "Yeah, I know Maddie," he said. He knew all the Conway girls. Everyone did who grew up in this town. Like him, they'd stuck around. But unlike him, they had better reasons for it.

Maddie was the youngest. A nice girl. A pretty girl, too, he thought, thinking of the auburn-haired young woman with the playful smile and sparkling grey eyes he occasionally saw laughing over drinks with one of her cousins or sisters at the pub.

"I can stop by the job site and give her an estimate," he said, but Candy's eyes went wide as she shook her head.

"Oh, I'm sure you'll be more than fair. That is if you're available?"

"I'm headed into town now to fix a faucet over at the post office," Cole said. "But my schedule's clear after that. I can swing by the bakery and start today, if Maddie agrees, of course," he added.

"Of *course*." Candy's eyes were wide. "She's usually there most of the day. Now, I won't keep you. I can see you're very busy, and I have to toddle along now. I help out at the café, you see. I make an *excellent* cheese biscuit, amongst other things." Her smile was far from humble, and Cole couldn't help but grin.

"Good to meet you, Candy. And thanks for considering me. I hope Maddie feels the same." He raised his eyebrows. It was obvious that Candy wasn't from this town originally. No one from Blue Harbor would be this eager to hire him, not unless Gus was tied up. There were a few, of course, who took a chance and let him prove himself. But not enough. Not that he could say he blamed them.

"Oh, I can't see any reason why she wouldn't!" Candy raised an eyebrow as her smile turned coy.

Cole just chuckled as he climbed into his truck. He could think of a few good reasons why Maddie wouldn't want to hire him for the job, because if he'd learned one thing by living in this town his entire life it was that you never escaped your past, no matter how damn hard you tried.

*

Maddie stood in the open space that was, technically, her bakery. The late morning sunlight streamed through the windows that framed three sides of space, one of which looked out onto a deck that she would soon share with Amelia's café, who shared the wall where her counter and, behind it, her kitchen would go.

Maddie checked her phone again, wondering if she should bug Gus again or assume he was too busy to take the job, or if he just hadn't gotten around to returning her message, and then, feeling her anxiety build, she stuffed her phone back into the pocket of her jeans and focused on the paint cards in front of her. There were so many color schemes she could go with. Yellow was a happy, cheerful color. Amelia's café was mostly blue, aside from the patio furniture, which she'd painted in yellow and pink, so blue was probably out.

Maddie held up a swatch of yellow to the wall that would house the counter and menu board.

"Too light," a voice behind her boomed.

She turned, startled to see a man standing in her open doorway, and not just any man. It was Cole McCarthy. Blue Harbor's resident bad boy, to be exact.

She blinked, not knowing what to even say, or where to even begin. "Excuse me?" she settled on, when really, what she wanted to ask was what the hell he was doing here, in her bakery of all places.

"We're not open for business yet," she said, with a tight smile.

He raised his eyebrows, had the nerve to look amused. "I think that's obvious."

Maddie looked around the space self-consciously. It was an empty space. Evidence of its previous occupant was still glaring, with holes in the walls where shelves had been, and dated brass light fixtures that were covered in dust.

Cole motioned to the paint swatch in her hand. "The sunlight will wash that out by high noon," he said, and she knew then that she wasn't imagining this. That Cole was standing in her bakery, giving his unsolicited opinions on her paint choices.

Before she could think of a rebuttal, he had crossed the room and was standing at her side, his big, tanned hands rifling through the stack of swatches that she'd collected from the local hardware store last week. He pulled another yellow strip from the pile and held it to the wall. He was so close that she could smell the musk of his skin, and sense the heat of another body in her space.

She inched to the side.

He nodded, pleased with what he saw. "This one's better," he said matter-of-factly and handed her the card.

Maddie took it, barely glancing at it, because really, what was he even doing here? Cole McCarthy had been a bully back in school—all twelve years of it (well, fourteen for him, since he'd repeated both third grade *and* fourth grade, landing him in her class eventually) from the time they were still playing in the sandbox to the moment they crossed the auditorium stage and received their high school diplomas—and since then he'd kept to himself, spotted around town, never with a smile, usually just a curt nod if any acknowledgment of anyone at all, sometimes spotted at a pub, sitting at the bar alone, drinking a beer while watching the game.

She hadn't seen him around in months. He wasn't one for community gatherings. And she hadn't spoken to him in years—and that had only been to ask him to pass her a pencil that had rolled under his desk in Calculus her senior year, and when he'd handed it to her, his dark eyes had bored through hers and she could have sworn she'd heard him growl.

"I appreciate your opinion," she said, trying her best to sound in control of this situation when she was pretty darn sure that Cole had the upper hand at the moment and when she absolutely did not appreciate his unsolicited advice. This was her bakery. All hers. Each of her sisters had been given an inheritance from their mother and she had saved hers for this day and applied her share of the prize money Amelia had given her for helping her win a recipe contest last month that had gotten the café some much-deserved press. This was *her* bakery! Her paint color to choose. Even if she was now doubting the color she had just been considering a few minutes earlier. Damn it!

"If you're looking for coffee or breakfast, you'll have to go next door to my sister's café."

His expression didn't change. Not even an inch. She stared into those dark eyes uneasily. They were very nice eyes, actually. His lashes were surprisingly long. But they gave nothing away.

"I'm not here for coffee," he finally said. "I'm here to work."

She coughed so she wouldn't laugh. She would eventually hire an assistant, but she wasn't at the point of interviewing yet, and she could hardly imagine Cole in an apron, mixing cookie dough.

"A woman named Candy approached me this morning?" His mouth quirked for one, telling second, and it was so brief, that Maddie might have missed it if she hadn't been staring at him in such complete and utter shock. "Said you needed a contractor for a build-out?"

"Oh." Maddie licked her lip and gave a nervous laugh. She would throttle Candy for this! "She's my father's girlfriend." That description still sounded weird, even after all these months. "She was trying to help, but...I've got it covered."

He raised an eyebrow. "Really? Okay, well, good to know."

"Yes," Maddie nodded. Mouth pinched. No nonsense here. Conversation over. "I'm all set. But...thank you."

Her heart was racing, and she was already thinking of

exactly what she would say to Candy the moment she got in touch with her. She began walking toward the door, leading Cole on his merry way, wanting to close the door and lock it behind him and retreat into her safe space. Her personal space. Her chosen space.

Really!

Cole turned when he reached the door. "So who'd you go with?"

Go with? Maddie blanked for a moment but then latched onto the first name she could think of. "Gus," she said. The most obvious.

Cole nodded slowly because of course this made complete sense. Everyone knew that Gus was the primary contractor in town. He'd been in business for decades. He was in high demand.

Very high demand, she'd come to realize.

Her stomach tightened when Cole cut her a look. "Interesting."

Maddie frowned, not sure what he meant by that. "Well, Gus has always done the work around our house, so…"

"I just saw him this morning," Cole said. "Stopped at the hardware store on the way to a job. He told me he was about to start a laundry list of projects this week. On your house."

"On my house?" Maddie squeaked. Her mind was spinning. Amelia wouldn't have hired him for anything, meaning that Cole must be referring to her childhood home. She tried to think of an excuse.

She tried to think of an explanation.

"Guess Candy approached him, too. Yesterday. Told me she was *very* persuasive. Offered him top dollar."

There was that quirk of his mouth again. There was no missing it this time.

Maddie swallowed hard. She thought fast, but her mind could only land on one thing. Or one person, rather. Candy.

"Well, I'm sure you'll get it all straightened out," Cole said. He tipped his chin and then walked down the steps, slowly disappearing up the path that led to Main Street.

Maddie stood in the open doorway, watching him go, wondering if he would turn back, and wondering if she should call after him. But that would be preposterous! Completely ridiculous! Something that she never would have chosen, and wouldn't accept.

She narrowed her eyes as she marched out the door and locked it behind her.

Candy had some explaining to do.

*

The Firefly Café was packed, as it always was, and Maddie felt a wave of longing as she entered. Was it only a matter of weeks ago that she was tying the blue and white striped apron strings at her waist and rolling out her cinnamon rolls? She still made two sheets of them every morning for Amelia, who collected them on her walk to work and then popped them into the oven.

Oh, to turn back time, to when life wasn't filled with uncertainty and pressure and stress. When she could chat and bake and laugh with her sister in the kitchen, working just as much in companionable silence as they did in camaraderie.

Amelia was at the counter, but the smile immediately slipped from her face when she saw Maddie's expression.

"Uh-oh. What happened?"

"Is Candy here?" Maddie asked.

Amelia raised an eyebrow but didn't press. "In the kitchen."

Maddie nodded, and then pushed through the swing door into the kitchen that felt so familiar, she almost got a little weepy. That was until she saw Candy, or rather the rump of her, bent over at the waist, pulling a tray from the lower oven.

She turned, looking pleasantly surprised to see Maddie standing at the big island. Maddie was sure to keep a safe distance between them, physically, lest she do something she would regret.

"Maddie! So good to see you! Couldn't stay away, huh?" She laughed loudly and then held out the tray. "Biscuit?"

Maddie shook her head. "I'm afraid we have a problem, Candy. Did you hire Gus to work for you so he wouldn't be available to work at the bakery?"

Candy's eyes widened for a moment, and she blinked slowly, clearly formulating her excuse.

"I sent a contractor over for you! Just as I promised I would. Was there…a problem?" She looked a little pale now.

"Yes, Candy, there was a problem." Maddie held her voice steady. Surely this could all be sorted out. Whatever

27

project Candy needed Gus for could wait. "I thought you were going to track down Gus for me. Get me on his schedule."

"Oh, but his schedule is all full right now," Candy said with a little smile.

"Doing work for you," Maddie said slowly.

"Well, amongst other things," Candy said quickly, but she couldn't meet Maddie's eye. "He said he was busy with small projects, couldn't take on anything bigger right now."

"Gus rarely does small projects. Maybe in the winter."

Candy huffed out a breath. "I'm just the messenger, Maddie! And I did find you a contractor."

"Cole McCarthy?" Maddie raised an eyebrow.

Candy's face lit up. "Handsome man, that Cole. You girls failed to mention that Sunday night."

"And you failed to mention that you had work that needed to be done at the house and couldn't wait," Maddie replied. It took everything in her not to point out that it wasn't even Candy's house. It was her house—at least, her father's. But it was home. It always would be.

Now Candy's cheeks were pink. Clearly, she wasn't going to talk her way out of this one. She glanced at the door, visibly relieved when Amelia came into the kitchen, carrying a plate of food, her cheeks flushed.

"Everything okay in here?" Amelia looked from Maddie to Candy.

"Just fine!" Candy trilled at the same time Maddie blurted, "No. Things are definitely not fine."

Candy looked stricken. Amelia looked worried.

"It's not Dad, is it?" she asked.

"Of course, not," Maddie said. "I would have told you first thing if it was about Dad." Though in some ways, Maddie supposed it was about their father. He'd urged Maddie to let Candy get involved, to help, and now Maddie realized she would have been much better off handling things on her own.

"Good, because table four just sent back their order. Said there weren't enough apples today."

She set down the dish of her signature apple stuffed French toast and Maddie took a moment to look at it. "Looks like plenty of apples to me."

"Well, if the customer isn't happy, I'll have to remake it and quickly. Candy, can you please cover the dining room for a moment?"

Candy needed no further encouragement as she darted from the room.

Maddie let the argument slide while she watched Amelia dredge four thick slices of bread in the pre-made egg mixture and fry it in butter, before making two sandwiches from it, with the cinnamon and brown-sugar-coated apples melting inside.

She resisted the urge to offer to help, knowing that Amelia would send her away, as she had any time that Maddie offered her services since giving her notice, but when Candy returned with another order slip a few minutes later, Maddie saw her chance.

"Want me to get started on that?"

"Nope." Amelia chuckled under her breath as Maddie felt her shoulders deflate.

"I'm right here, and I'm happy to help."

"You have your own business to worry about now, Maddie," Amelia replied as she plated the French toast and drizzled it with fresh caramel sauce. "Besides, this is nothing. I'm used to putting out fires."

"And you make it look so easy," Maddie said, realizing now that it couldn't always be so easy. That if she had an upset customer and had to remake an order while also tending to new customers, she wasn't sure she could do it quite as effortlessly as Amelia.

"It all comes with training and time. You'll see. It just takes a little practice, and…a little confidence. And when all else fails, trust your instincts. Go with your gut. It's usually right."

Trust her instincts. She would try to do just that.

Amelia gave her a little wink and scooted out of the room. A second later, Candy reappeared.

Maddie crossed her arms firmly across her chest. Candy did her best to feign innocence as she rinsed the French toast pan in the sink.

"Now," Amelia said, reappearing again. "You were saying?"

"Maddie isn't pleased with the contractor I found to do her bakery," Candy said a little pertly.

Amelia slid her gaze to Maddie, her brow pinching. "Who is it?"

Now it was Maddie's turn to look smug. "Cole McCarthy."

Amelia bit down on her lip, clearly in an effort to hide a smile. She didn't need to say anything. They were both thinking the same thing. Of course Candy had hired Cole, a young bachelor, to do the project, instead of good old Gus. Of course she had!

"Well, he's probably cheaper than Gus," Amelia pointed out. Practical, that sister of hers.

Maddie begrudgingly agreed but said nothing.

"And if it gets the job done, does it really matter who does it?"

Again, with the rational points.

"Fine," Maddie blurted, narrowing her eyes in Candy's direction.

Candy just feigned disinterest and scurried to the door. "Better get these biscuits plated!"

Maddie watched her go and then slowly turned back to her sister, who was having a good, hard laugh at her expense.

"Hey," she said, holding up her hands and backing up. "Candy did what she promised, right? She got you a contractor. Problem solved."

Maddie pushed miserably through the door, unable to even comment further on this bizarre twist of events. Contrary to what Amelia might think, her problems were far from solved.

Now she would have to track down Cole McCarthy and see if he'd be willing to come back. And from the way they'd left things off, there was no denying that he wasn't going to make any part of it easy for her.

3

Maddie didn't know Cole's number, but she knew where he lived—an innocent enough looking house that had somehow been the setting of local lore for most of her childhood. That was Cole's turf back then, and Maddie and Cora, who was only a year ahead of her in school, would approach the bus stop each morning apprehensively, their cheerful conversation drawing to a halt when they caught sight of the boy who seemed to always be angry, whether it meant brooding on the curb, not making direct eye contact with anyone, or picking up rocks and chucking them down the road, as if he had a target in mind. Once, before Maddie knew better, she'd tried to cheer him up, because that's what she did around the house, and it usually worked. When her mother got sick, she learned that drawing pictures and cards would always bring a smile to her mother's face, no matter how bad she was feeling that day. She would admire the drawing, often with tears in her eyes, and then tuck it into her bedside table drawer, along with all the others.

Maddie didn't make a card for Cole because she suspected as a boy he wouldn't appreciate her drawings of flowers and rainbows and butterflies, but her mother had always told her that Maddie could turn even the greyest day into sunshine with her smile, so Maddie decided to go with that. Cole was sitting on the curb that morning; the bus was running late. As usual, he spoke to no one, greeted no one, looked at no one. It was spring. It was warm. And personally, Maddie was hoping that by the time school let out for the day, she might be able to convince her mother to let her take a dip in the lake, even though she knew the water would be icy cold. What was Cole so bent out of shape about? She walked close to where he was perched, watching him until she caught his eye (and oh, it was a menacing stare, causing her to almost lose her nerve), and then she smiled, a big, hopeful smile, and said, "It's a nice sunny day, don't you think?"

Her smile slipped when she saw the set of his jaw and he stood, making her take a step back, and then picked up his faded navy backpack with its fraying straps and walked to the other side of the street, even though it meant he would have to cross back over again when the bus finally arrived.

Maddie supposed it could have been worse. The next week at school he had slammed a kid named Dwight into a locker for reasons no one ever did know, gotten a two-day suspension for it.

From that day on, Maddie kept her distance.

But today, she would have to seek him out.

With a heavy sigh, Maddie gathered up her paint samples and considered her dilemma. Cole was a contractor, and he was available, and she did need the work done.

She looked at the paint color she had chosen and held it to the wall like she had earlier. Now, the natural sunlight was brighter, filling the entire room in its golden glow. And just like Cole had said, the color faded away. On an entire wall, it would be lost.

She pursed her lips. If she was going to get the project going, she was going to have to choose a paint color soon. And she may as well entertain the idea of a slightly brighter shade…

Maddie gathered up her belongings and walked to the hardware store, telling herself that she wasn't really delaying reaching out to Cole. She could stop by Cole's house at the end of the day when he'd be home. She could pay her father a visit afterward, too. Have a little chat about Candy's behavior. Or maybe, she could find another contractor by then—someone from a neighboring town, someone who happened to be available to start within the next few days.

But each day she pushed the work back, she also delayed her opening. And with each day that she wasn't open, she was losing money. Bills were still due, regardless of whether she had an empty space or a bustling business.

Her anxiety flared up again as she stuffed the paint swatches into her tote and caught sight of her notepad, covered in furious scribbles of her ideas and lists, but she focused on the task at hand. Today she would commit to a paint color. She would check that box off her list and it would feel great. It was the most basic of her tasks, but the decision still felt all important. She wanted every detail of this bakery to be just right. She just wasn't as confident with her decision-making as Amelia—or Britt or Cora.

She walked down the aisles she was now vaguely familiar with since she first started coming in here a couple of weeks ago when her plans for the space began to take shape. The display of paint swatches lined the back wall like a rainbow spread out before her, and all at once, she was met with indecision again. Her mind flitting from yellow to green and lingering on the blue. But no, no blue. She had already decided that. She didn't want to copy Amelia. She wanted to be her own person. She wanted the bakery to be her own space.

But leave it to Amelia to have picked the best color.

Still, yellow complimented blue, and the establishments would be linked through an open doorway and a shared patio. Feeling surer of her decision, she focused on the endless shades of yellow, wondering how she would ever choose the correct one, when a hand came up beside her, plucked a strip, and handed it over.

She looked over to see Cole standing beside her, one eyebrow cocked in a way that was almost mocking and almost nonplussed.

"I see you decided to take my advice."

She jutted her chin, wanting to tell him that no, she had not taken his advice, she was simply considering all her options, but she knew from the glint in his dark eyes that there was no point in denying it.

"I saw your point about that particular color being too subtle."

His mouth twitched. She narrowed her eyes. Pulled in a breath, forced herself to get through what she was about to say next.

"I'm glad that we ran into each other."

Now his expression was one of undeniable disbelief. Okay, so *glad* was probably a bit of a stretch. Still, it saved her the trouble of hunting him down. Going to that house that was hidden behind a wall of overgrown shrubs, the curtains always pulled, rumors of it being haunted always whispered amongst the kids on the school bus.

Maddie had never thought the house was haunted. She'd thought it was sad, despite the yellow paint. Whereas her own house always had a cheerful wreath on the door, pumpkins lining its porch steps for Halloween, and garland and lights for Christmas, Cole's house had looked the same year-round. It looked unhappy. As unhappy as the boy who lived there.

"I was, uh, wondering if you'd still be up for the project."

He didn't look surprised when he asked, "What about Gus?"

She had known he wouldn't make this easy. She shrugged and said, "Seems that he's taken another job after all." She refused to admit that he was right about this, too. "And I need someone to start on this soon."

He nodded, seemed to mull something over for what felt like an unbearable amount of time. Eventually, he said, "Lots of people are trying to fit in projects before the winter hits. It's a busy time of year."

"You weren't busy this morning," she pointed out. Was he seriously going to claim he couldn't take on the project? Her heart began to hammer in her chest, and she swallowed hard, hoping that the desperation hadn't registered on her face.

He motioned to his cart, which held multiple cans of paint. "Big project has come up. Painting the exterior of a house."

"That just came up today? In the…two hours since I last saw you?"

He didn't say anything, just shrugged.

"Look, I'm sorry if we got off to a…bad start this morning," Maddie said quickly. "Candy had mentioned that she would help line up Gus for the work and so it came as a…a *surprise* when you came into the bakery."

"A surprise, eh? And not a pleasant one," Cole said, and it was then that she noticed his eyes had gone a little flat. The glimmer of amusement was lost.

"I was caught off guard," she explained. "That was all."

She held her breath, wondering if he would turn her down, knowing that he had the full advantage here. There was no doubt that Candy had painted the full picture for him: told him exactly when she needed the project completed, knowing that Gus was otherwise occupied, thanks to her. Could she find someone in a neighboring town to help out? Probably. But on such a compressed timeline, that was unlikely.

"I'll be there at six," Cole said, so gruffly that she barely caught what he'd said.

She blinked, hurrying after him as he walked toward the cashier. "Six? Tonight?" Not that she had other plans, but at the market on Sunday, her cousin Gabby had mentioned maybe meeting for dinner tonight, if she finished all her flower deliveries in time.

Cole set two of the paint cans on the counter. "Six in the morning."

Maddie was used to getting up early—after all, up until last month, she would walk with Amelia to the café each morning at five, to get a start on the day before the café doors opened at seven. But this just felt so…sudden.

Still, his demeanor told her that there would be room for discussion. "I'll see you then," she said, with a nod.

He held her gaze until she was forced to look away. She clutched her paint strips in her hand and marched out the door, only breathing a sigh of relief once her feet hit the sidewalk, but knowing that it was short-lived.

Really, if she'd known just how difficult it would be to start her own business, she wasn't so sure she would have ever taken the plunge!

*

That night Maddie sat across from Gabby at a high-top table at the pub in the Carriage House Inn, one of the more popular establishments on Main Street that had been owned by the Bradford family for generations. The eldest son, Jackson, was tending bar, and more than once Maddie had caught a telling glance pass between him and her cousin.

"Why don't you just admit you like him?" she finally said, because hey, today wasn't the day to be dancing around the obvious, was it? She'd seen firsthand the way that her father and then Amelia had run their businesses over the years, and she knew that Cora was much the same, feeling confident in how she handled everything from displays to purchasing to customers. Britt was probably the toughest of them all, because of the no-nonsense approach she'd garnered from working in management consulting before returning to town. Maddie would have to learn to be in control, rather than sit back and let her sisters drive her decisions, as they always had. And she would have to do that starting tomorrow.

God help her.

She took another sip of her wine. It was one of her family's blends, sold in many restaurants in town. She'd feel traitorous drinking anything else, and she knew that Gabby felt the same way, seeing as her own father had been co-owner of the orchard until his retirement a couple of years ago.

But Gabby wasn't drinking her wine. Right now she was giving Maddie a hard look.

"I do *not* have a thing for Jackson Bradford," she said firmly. "The guy is a complete cad."

True, all true. Jackson had a charming—if not flirtatious—demeanor that wasn't reserved for just one special someone. He'd dated a lot of the girls in town before moving on to the tourists who flocked to the area each summer. And he wasn't shy about his intentions to stay unattached. He couldn't be more different than his younger brother Robbie, who had been devoted to Britt for years before circumstances drove them apart, leaving him a widower and a single dad. And even he was still willing to try again, now happily reunited with his high school sweetheart.

Still, both Amelia and Maddie had suspected there was some attraction between Gabby and Jackson for years. She gave her cousin a little shrug. Gabby was beautiful, always had been, and Jackson was easily one of the best-looking bachelors in town.

Make that one of the only bachelors in town, she thought with a sigh.

"Would it be so unreasonable to assume that you might find him good-looking?" With his dark hair and killer smile, it was almost a statement of fact that Jackson was attractive.

"Of course he's good-looking," Gabby said lightly. She speared her salad and said, "But lots of men are."

"In this town?" Maddie almost laughed. They'd grown up with the same group, gone through each grade seeing the same faces. Half those people had left town upon high school graduation, and the ones that stayed...Well, the pickings were a bit slim, especially when you eliminated any guy who had ever so much as kissed a sister or cousin or friend.

"Sure," Gabby said. "The Bradfords are a fine-looking bunch."

"And two of them are spoken for," Maddie pointed out, referring to Robbie and their cousin Matt—Amelia's boyfriend. "Gage doesn't even live in Blue Harbor," she added, though she wondered if now that Matt had returned to town, his younger brother might follow.

"And I always thought Cole McCarthy was attractive, in that mysterious, brooding type of way."

Maddie almost choked on her drink, and she let out a

small cough to cover her surprise. She set her glass down carefully and looked at her cousin across the table, wondering what she knew and what she was playing at. But Gabby just poked at her salad. Clearly, word hadn't spread to the flower shop.

Yet.

"Cole McCarthy," she repeated, incredulous. "You think that *Cole* is good-looking?"

Her mind flashed back to the way his eyes had lingered on hers, seeming to look right into the depths of her soul, reading her every thought, until she'd been forced to look away. She shivered now, just thinking about it.

"Hell yeah!" Gabby gave her a quizzical look. "With those deep-set dark eyes and that thick, dark hair. He's so…quiet. So…intense."

"So unfriendly," Maddie said, jabbing at her own salad. "That's what he is."

Gabby gave a little smile. "I'd like to say he's more…mysterious."

Maddie snorted. "You've been reading too many of those romance novels that Bella orders for you."

Gabby's cousin on her mother's side owned the town's only bookstore and kept her loyal patrons' favorite authors stocked. Maddie knew for certain that the romance section of her shop had expanded due to Gabby's patronage.

And lately, Candy's, too.

"What can I say? I'm a romantic." Gabby grinned. "I should be, considering I sell flowers for a living. Oh, and while we are on the topic of my beloved reading material, I wanted to invite you to book club this Saturday night."

Maddie had always seen the signs for Bella's monthly book club that was held at her bookstore across the street from Gabby's shop, and she knew that Gabby never missed a meeting. Maddie had never been able to go since Saturday nights at the café were usually so busy, but now she couldn't think of an excuse.

"Okay!" She smiled.

"Boy, you didn't need to think about that for long," Gabby said, laughing.

It was true. Some decisions were easy, and once you committed, it was easier to follow through than hem and haw.

"I've wanted to go for a while to support Bella's business." Although…a flashback of a conversation with Candy came to mind. "Doesn't Candy attend those meetings?"

"Only once," Gabby said. She fought off a smile. "She brought her cheese biscuits."

Maddie laughed. "Of course she did. Well, I'll bring pie. Of course. And maybe something from my new menu."

"Good idea!" Gabby licked her lip. "Brownies?"

Maddie had been trying to perfect her brownie recipe, so she nodded. "It's a plan."

Gabby pulled a paperback from her bag and slid it across the table. "I already finished, so you can use my copy. And speaking of businesses, how is the bakery coming along? Do you have a set opening date?"

Like her sisters, Gabby was a successful small business owner, but unlike her sisters, Maddie didn't feel the same need to keep up with her. She sighed and wondered how much she wanted to open up tonight. In some ways, it was nice to get her mind off things for a little while.

"It's all a little overwhelming," she admitted, her heart starting to pick up speed. "At the café, I pretty much just did what Amelia asked."

Gabby tipped her head, giving her a look of understanding. "You've had years of hands-on training between the orchard and working for Amelia. Once you get things running, you'll be fine."

"I hope so," Maddie said. She inhaled deeply.

"You could always ask Britt for advice if you're not sure about something," Gabby said. "I'm sure she'd love to give you some advice."

As a former management consultant, Britt would, and she would also know what she was talking about it, too, but Britt almost knew too much when it came to operating a successful business, and she was a little intimidating at times. Maddie thought back to the spring when Britt was eager for her to mass-produce her pies at the family orchard, not understanding easily that not everything Maddie did was for profit. Baking came from her heart.

"It will be fine once I get things off the ground," she said, hoping that was true. "I think I'll feel more excited once it starts to actually look like a bakery. Construction starts tomorrow."

"You using Gus?"

Maddie braced herself for it. "No. He's unavailable. I'm using…well, Cole, actually."

As expected, Gabby's eyes widened. "Is that so?"

"It's not like that," Maddie said, frowning. "My dad wanted me to let Candy be involved in the bakery. She's so eager to help us, to be a part of our lives." The cousins exchanged a knowing look. "And when she suggested she line up the contractor, it felt like a win-win at the time."

"I'll say it did!" Gabby laughed.

Maddie bit down on her teeth, still mad every time she thought of Candy's part in all of this. "Well, it's only for a couple of weeks," she said, trying to make herself feel better. It couldn't drag on longer than that—not if she wanted to get her doors open by October, and not if she wanted to keep her sanity, either.

"A lot can happen in a couple of weeks," Gabby said, waggling her eyebrows.

Maddie was in no mood. "Now you sound like Candy."

"I'll take that as a compliment," Gabby said with a grin. "We both have your best interest at heart."

"And you think that Cole McCarthy is in my best interest?" Maddie shook her head. "The only thing that's going to transpire in the next couple of weeks is the build-out of my space."

"If you say so," Gabby remarked.

"I do say so," Maddie said. More than that, she knew so.

Gabby was ahead of Cole in school. She hadn't seen his daily antics in class, hadn't known the trouble he'd caused. Hadn't stood beside him at the bus stop every day, feeling on edge, knowing that his every move was so unpredictable.

And that in many ways, it still was. Gabby may have been correct in describing Cole as mysterious, but while her cousin may find that sort of thing appealing, Maddie did not.

Maddie wanted safety, stability, and security from relationships, and from her business.

She'd had enough upheaval to last a lifetime.

4

Cole was already sitting in the back of the truck, the hatch down, when Maddie arrived at one minute to six the next morning, holding two thermoses of hot coffee, which she hoped might lessen the tension that she sensed was still lingering between them. Not only that, but she'd spent so much time getting ready for what should have been a regular day planning menus and ordering supplies that she hadn't had time to enjoy her coffee at home, and it seemed rude to only bring something for herself.

She extended a thermos to him. He took it with a nod.

"You were sure that I'd show," he remarked.

It was true that a part of her had wondered if he'd bail, disappear, or change his mind. She'd lost count of how many times he'd cut class back in school. Attendance was hardly one of his strong points.

"I took a chance," she said. A lot of chances. Everything about opening this business had started to feel like one big chance. One big risk.

He took a sip, hopped out of the back of the truck, and grabbed his toolbox with his free hand.

Her gaze drifted to the cords in his arms as his muscles tensed. Despite the chill in the air, he was wearing a tee shirt and jeans, and if the temperature bothered him, he didn't show it.

"Good coffee," was all he said as he walked to the bakery.

Maddie fished her key from her tote and unlocked the door. Every time she entered the bare space her heart swelled with excitement. She'd never had anything that was just hers before. Being the youngest of four sisters, she was used to wearing hand-me-downs that had made it from Britt to Amelia to Cora and to her without being completely threadbare. The house she now lived in technically belonged to Amelia, and she was just renting out the bottom unit, and despite Amelia being too kind to ever admit she was cutting her a deal, Maddie knew what real estate went for around here, and she knew that she was being taken care of, much the same as she'd been brought on to the café, and was still welcome to help out at the orchard. Cora would no doubt hire her without a blink of an eye either.

She was lucky. She was grateful. And now it was time to prove that she didn't need help. She could do this all on her own.

Only question was, could she? The doubts were still there, even as she rolled out the blueprints (again, kindly drawn up by Amelia's boyfriend) and walked Cole through the space.

They landed in the large room that had once been used for storage and overstock. "This will be the kitchen," she explained. It was a big room, with shelving and cabinets. There had been no need for a kitchen in a stationery store. "This wall backs up to the kitchen of the café, so the plumbing and gas lines should all be easily accessible."

At least, that's what Matt had told her when he drew up the plans and approved her permits.

The room had been cleared out, but still, it felt suddenly claustrophobic, despite its fairly generous size. Cole was blocking the doorway, a strange, large physical presence in what had up until now been an empty four walls that echoed when she walked.

She swallowed hard, not sure what to say next, knowing that she was technically in charge here and that he was probably waiting for her to take the lead. That there was no Amelia to turn to, or Britt, or her father for that matter.

She cleared her throat, about to ask about supplies when she heard the main door swing open. "Yoohoo!" a voice called out from the other room.

Oh, brother.

"Candy." Maddie's eyes hooded, and for a moment, she felt a secret exchange pass between her and Cole when he cocked an eyebrow.

Just as quickly, it was gone, and he stepped aside, letting her pass, back into the storefront, where sure enough, Candy was standing near the windows, in head to toe pink aside from the blue and white striped apron that she wore from the café, bearing a basket of her "famous" cheese biscuits, which she'd managed to convince Amelia to offer at the café.

She set the basket down on the card table that Maddie had set up her first day here as a makeshift desk, and opened her arms wide, coming toward Maddie with a look that was nearing apologetic, until her eyes darted to the storage room door and landed on Cole.

Her expression transformed to one of transparent joy, and she clasped her hands together, shooting coy looks at Maddie that were anything but subtle.

"Cole! So you're here! Oh, I'm so happy that this is working out. I just knew that this arrangement would be perfect."

"Did you now?" Maddie leveled a stare at Candy, who did a masterful job of ignoring her.

Instead, she reached for her basket, proffering it to Cole as she explained, "I brought you some goodies. Nothing special, just my world-famous cheese biscuits." She laughed until she snorted. "After all, a *big, strong* young man like yourself is probably going to work up quite an appetite with all this *manual* labor."

Maddie resisted an eye roll. Cole, to his credit, took the basket and managed something that almost classified as an actual smile. "These look delicious. Thank you, Candy."

Now Maddie felt herself frown. What was this? The man was being more polite to her father's pushy girlfriend than he was to her, his employer?

Granted, they had gotten off to a rather strange start. And Candy was a force. Perhaps he just knew what he was dealing with, and that it was easier to let her have her way.

Or perhaps he was just being nice…

She shook that thought away. Cole McCarthy was a recluse. A broody, moody man. He wasn't mysterious. He was unfriendly.

Mostly.

"Well," Candy said, giving Maddie a suggestive look. "I'll let you two get back to…whatever it was that I interrupted." She waggled her eyebrows, biting down on her bottom lip in excitement.

"You mean the kitchen plans?" Maddie folded her arms across her chest.

"If that's what you're calling it!" Candy grinned as she inched away. She glanced back once more to rake her eyes over Cole before disappearing out the door. Still, she could be seen looking through the windows as she crossed the deck back toward the café.

Cole set a hand on the wall near where the counter would be. "You're positive that you want a doorway here connecting your bakery to the café?" he asked, and Maddie turned to him, surprised, and burst out laughing.

That was odd, she realized, immediately composing herself. Laughing at something Cole McCarthy had said? Cole didn't make people laugh. He made people squirm.

"Candy isn't a permanent hire," she replied. At least, she didn't think so, and she doubted Amelia did either. But Candy may have other plans, and Candy tended to get her way, didn't she? "And it will be good for business," she added.

Still, she now had visions of Candy floating through the open entrance at her every whim, pulling Maddie in for long, squishy hugs, and embarrassing her in front of her customers.

Business would slow, she reminded herself. With Amelia's seasonal help gone, and Maddie too, it made sense for Candy to stay on through the fall.

Except that Maddie had been a year-round employee, hadn't she?

She set a hand on her stomach. "Really, Candy is the least of my problems," she told Cole. "I still have to place the order for furniture for this place and hire an assistant." And about a hundred other things, too.

Her heart sped up. She took a sip of coffee, wishing it was something stronger.

"The kitchen is the top priority, though," she was sure to mention.

"You know I have some thoughts about your kitchen," Cole said as he leafed through the printed descriptions of the fixtures and appliances that she had already chosen. He pulled his measuring tape from his back pocket and disappeared into the storage room.

Reluctantly, Maddie followed. She had painstakingly chosen every last detail, down to the exact backsplash tile, comparing each item against her budget ten times over, so she was sure not to spend too much. With her opening date scheduled in a little over two weeks, now was not the time to be changing her plan.

Or doubting herself further.

Still, she had waited to place any orders until she had her contractor approve her final plans, and seeing as Cole was now filling that role, she supposed she should hear him out.

Cole consulted the blueprints that Matt had drawn up and double-checked the measurements of the wall that was meant to house the pantry. "If you're willing to cut back on some cabinet space, you could fit two extra ovens right here, with a small cabinet on top."

Maddie felt herself waver. And she didn't want to waver. Extra ovens would speed up production, especially since she expected her staff to be lean, but that also meant more money and less storage space.

"I'd rather just stick with the plan." Her stomach was starting to hurt.

"I'm just pointing out that it's something to consider," Cole said with a shrug. "But it's your call. I'm just thinking of efficiency."

"And where am I supposed to store all my supplies?" She thought of the items she would order in bulk from Amelia's trusted suppliers: sugar, flour, salt, and other dry goods.

"We could easily build out this broom closet for a second pantry," Cole said, crossing the room and pulling open a door. "I could customize the shelving." He looked at her for approval.

Maddie was not used to anyone looking to her for approval. They looked at Amelia. Or growing up, Britt, then Amelia, then Cora. Never Maddie.

Maddie put her hands to her forehead, not liking where this was going. The plans had been set. Painstakingly so. Now was the time to commit to them, not doubt them.

"I'm on a budget," Maddie said. She wrung her hands, now imaging how increasing her oven space would increase productivity and make her mornings move a little quicker.

Cole snapped his measuring tape back into place. "Let me see what I can work out with your supplier. Contractor rates and all."

Maddie felt touched. And humbled. "Thank you," she said softly.

Cole shrugged, not making eye contact. "Just doing my job. Keeping the boss happy." He walked out of the storage room, and before she could even make it to the main room, opened the front door. "I'll head out for supplies and get started. I can probably get those extra ovens delivered with the rest of your order if we call them today. In the meantime, I can get started with the rest of the build-out."

"Any chance that the kitchen will be somewhat usable by the end of next week?"

Cole gave her a long look. "I thought the place wasn't opening until the weekend after that."

"It isn't," Maddie explained. "But the Harvest Fest is next weekend and I'm hosting a stand. Amelia offered to let me use her kitchen at the café for all the baking, but it would be a lot better for everyone if I had my own space."

She'd taken enough of her sister's generosity for a lifetime, and all she wanted was to finally have something all of her own.

She just hadn't realized how difficult that would be.

"I'll see what I can do," was all Cole said.

Maddie nodded and watched him go, leaving her standing alone in the middle of her bakery, thinking that Cole McCarthy wasn't quite as bad as she'd remembered him.

And that maybe Candy had helped her out after all. Not that she'd ever admit it.

*

"That you, Cole?"

Cole set his keys down on the small table in the front hall, wondering who else it could be, but knowing that even now, a good twenty years after his father had upped and left town, his mother was still holding out hope that Karl McCarthy would walk in the door and sit down at the dinner table as if nothing had ever happened.

His mother was good at pretending that everything was okay. Always was, even back when he was just a kid and he could see the pain in her eyes, see the beer bottles in the trash that she tried to hide under paper towels, hear the door slam when his father came home late at night, or his mother pacing the creaking floors of her bedroom when he didn't come home at all.

She was always good at pretending everything was okay. Then and now. And just like now, when she tried to bite her lip to stifle the pain he knew she was experiencing, he felt something build up inside of him. Frustration. Anger. He couldn't help her, no matter how hard he tried.

The only difference between then and now was that he was a grown man, not a scrappy, helpless kid. He'd learned how to curb his emotions. Learned to hide them much the way his mother had. Knew his limitations. Accepted his lot.

His mother wasn't going to get any better this time. Every doctor he'd taken her to had said the same thing. And all he could do was try and make every day he had with her a little easier. Keep a roof over their heads. Pay off the mounting bills that came in every month from her treatments. Pick up her pain meds. Sometimes some flowers too.

He didn't like to get them at the flower shop in town, though. Instead, he gathered her favorite blooms from the garden, sticking them in vases around the house, or picking up something nice from the grocery store, where he wouldn't have to deal with Gabby Conway getting up in his business.

Not that there was anything wrong with Gabby. She was a nice girl. Pretty too. But she knew about as much as anyone could about people's business. Professional hazard. She knew who was having a birthday, and who had some apologizing to do. She knew who was about to get engaged. And who was sick.

No, better to keep it simple. No middle-men. No cards. No questions. Or rumors.

"It's me, Mom," he called out. He slipped off his work boots and walked to the kitchen, where she was sitting at the table, sipping a mug of tea. Their next-door neighbor was sitting in his usual chair, not that he minded. She stopped by at least once a week, always bringing cookies, sometimes dinner, offering to tidy up, and always putting a smile on his mother's face.

Today, his mother looked in better spirits. Her cheeks had color in them, and she seemed to sit a little straighter than usual. Immediately, he felt his shoulders relax.

"Hello, Janice," he said to the other woman. "How's Chris doing?"

Chris has moved to Philly years back and didn't visit as much as Janice would have liked, he knew. He'd been friends with Chris when they were kids—or as close as a friend as he had. Pushing people away had always been second nature, but his mother and Chris's mother had pushed the boys together, and Janice had seen to it that her son invited Cole fishing or out to swim on those long summer days when he was too young to work and school was out of session, and his mother was worried that he'd get into trouble.

And trouble he did.

Now, shame tore through him when he thought of the worry he'd caused her. The way her expression would fold every time he got sent home from school or the principal called, summoning her for another meeting. He'd do anything to take it all back, to undo the additional unhappiness he'd caused her.

For now, some roses would have to do.

"My, you're spoiled, Myrna," Janice marveled as she stood to fill a vase with water. She knew her way around the kitchen, and Cole had grown to like having her in the house. For so long it had just been him and his mother, and a change in dynamic was always good. It had just taken him a long time to learn that human connection could be a good thing.

"It's getting chilly out there," Cole observed. "I'm going to put a fresh coat of paint on the house the moment I wrap up my project."

"Cole is the contractor for the new bakery," his mother informed Janice.

Janice set the vase on the center of the table and resumed her spot. "I'd heard that Maddie Conway was opening a spot next to her sister's café. Wasn't she in the same grade as you?" She sipped her tea, but Cole didn't fail to notice the little glance she exchanged with his mother.

"She was," he grunted. Eventually. "Think I'll go shower now."

"Oh, but don't leave us hanging. When is the bakery opening?"

Cole paused in the doorway to the hall. He knew damn well that these two women were more interested in him working with Maddie than when the bakery would open. But seeing the light in his mother's eyes, he decided to humor her.

"A couple of weeks," he said. He hesitated and then decided to throw them another bone. "It's a real nice place she has planned."

And it was, or at least it would be. He'd make sure of that. He could see the potential. He wanted it to be a success. Maddie deserved that.

"Her mother was an angel," Janice remarked, clucking her tongue sadly. "Always kept that house just so, especially at Christmastime, do you remember?"

Cole's mother nodded sadly. "She was always sure to wave and smile. She was a good neighbor."

Janice shook her head. "She would be really proud of those girls. It's so sad that she's not here to see it."

A look passed between his mother and Cole, and he felt his jaw set, just as it always did when he thought of the reality of their circumstances. Still, he couldn't quite believe it. A part of him still hoped for a miracle, he supposed. That one day she'd get better. That the doctors had been wrong.

That his father would walk through that front door, just as his mother had always hoped he would.

"What does she plan to call it?" Janice asked, clearly not willing to let him go just yet.

Cole scratched his jaw. "I didn't ask. But thanks for the reminder. She'll need to get a sign up, and I'll have to be the one to hang it."

He gave them a little smile and excused himself, leaving them to enjoy their conversation and tea, and as he climbed the stairs to the bedroom he'd lived in all his life, he smiled at the sound of his mother's laughter, even if he couldn't help noticing that they were still on the subject of Maddie Conway, and what a pretty girl she'd always been.

5

Maddie had spent all of Thursday scouring antique stores across the county for the dishes for the shop. Remembering her mother's special tea party china had sparked an idea, and by Friday morning, she had two boxes of mix-matched plates, tea cups, and even three stunning hand-painted cake stands carefully wrapped and packed in the trunk of Amelia's car, which Amelia let Maddie borrow whenever she needed it—which was rare, but certainly handy these days. It wasn't exactly modern and fresh, but each piece told a story, and she liked to think that it would be something others would remember, years from now, just as she thought of those tea parties with her sisters.

She carried the first box gingerly into the bakery on Friday morning, hoping to load them into the storage closet, and clean and organize them while Cole worked. The existing bathroom was only getting a new coat of paint, and the sink was in full working order for this sort of activity. Plus, she probably needed to keep an eye on the guy. Given his history, she half doubted he'd even shown up to the job yesterday while she was away, and she was a little surprised to see his truck parked on the gravel path when she arrived.

When she walked into the empty space, the sound of hammering greeted her, and she was pleased to see that the floorboards had been covered with a protective layer of paper and tape and that three shades of sunshine yellow paint were marked in neat squares on each wall, so she could see how they caught the light throughout the day.

Blinking in awe, she set the box of dishes on the floor in the corner where they wouldn't be at risk of being tripped over and hesitantly made her way through the doorway to the kitchen, gasping at what she saw.

The storage space had been stripped out, the wall to the large closet had been broken down, and a new frame had been erected in its place for the smaller closet, allowing for more storage space and the extra ovens. It hadn't been in Matt's original design, and Maddie had been worried how Amelia or Matt would respond to that, until she told herself the entire drive back to Blue Harbor yesterday that it was her business and her decision.

And she'd always had Amelia's support. It was part of the reason she was so determined to do this on her own, without asking for any more help or generosity on her family's part.

Now, as she looked at the changes to the kitchen, she was confident she had made the right decisions. There was a fresh coat of creamy white paint on the walls that immediately brightened the space, and a row of shelves was already hung on the short wall, where Maddie had planned to house all her mixing bowls for easy access.

Cole had read her notes. He seemed to almost be ahead of schedule.

And she was speechless.

Cole stood with his back to her, putting the last of the shelves into place. His shoulders strained against the fabric of his blue tee shirt, and Maddie hung back a moment to admire his muscular form. She could almost see what Gabby had been saying the other night about Cole being easy on the eye. Almost.

Noticing her, he turned, his brow furrowing in concentration. "Didn't hear you come in. If you sneak up on me like that, I might end up dropping something next time. Don't need a hammer on my foot."

Well, so much for a friendly greeting. Maddie felt all her goodwill slip away.

"We never discussed those shelves, did we?" She motioned to the shelves, already envisioning her colorful bowls arranged on their surfaces.

His brow hooded. "No. I read the plans. Why?"

She smiled. "I'm just surprised is all. You've done more than I expected!"

His expression turned wary, as if he wasn't sure she'd paid him a compliment or not. He picked up his toolbox and slid a screwdriver back into its proper place. He was neat and thorough, she realized, watching him.

"What did you expect? That I'd be sitting around, taking a cigarette break every fifteen minutes?" He managed his first grin of the day, but even it was gone so quickly she'd barely caught it.

She felt guilty that this thought had, in fact, crossed her mind.

"Don't worry. I don't smoke. And the way I see it, the

sooner I get the job done, the sooner we're both able to get on with things, right?"

Now she was the one who wasn't so sure if he was insulting her or not. "That eager to get away from me, huh?"

He glanced her way, then back at the toolbox. "Never said that."

Silence fell. Maddie told herself not to read into anything.

"Look," she said, realizing that a formal apology was in order here. "I'm sorry that we got off on the wrong foot. I…" She hesitated, not quite sure how to finish that thought without making things worse, and that was certainly the last thing she wanted to do. Cole was right. She did want this project finished, and as quickly as possible, too.

He held up a hand. "Don't worry. I get it."

She studied him. "You do?"

He shrugged. "I have a reputation in this town. I'm not completely unaware of what people say about me, you know."

"Oh." Shame weighed on her as she searched for the best thing to say to smooth this all over. "I don't know about that…"

He cocked an eyebrow. She resisted a smile and failed.

"Don't worry about it, Maddie. I get it."

Did he? From the hurt that seemed to steep in his dark eyes, she wasn't so sure about that, but there was no room to push further, and it was clear that Cole didn't think so either. He jutted his chin to the main room. "What did you think of those paint colors?"

Maddie was relieved for the change of subject as she wandered back into the front room, aware of Cole's tread close behind her. For some reason, she wondered what her rear looked like in her jeans, and she wondered if she should have worn a dress or something more flattering instead. It wasn't like she had time to work out these days, and she had been taste-testing a lot of new recipes…

But a dress? She shook that thought off immediately. Ridiculous! Cole was her contractor, not her boyfriend. Besides, he had a reputation. A bad one. Even he didn't deny it.

Besides, this was a construction site. Not a bakery.

Yet.

Still, she folded her arms over her chest and stood where her rear was shielded by the windows. The colors he had painted in a neat row were similar, and she had a sneaking suspicion this was some sort of test, like possibly they were all the same color and he was waiting for a "told you so" moment. But her mind kept drifting to one in particular, and whether he liked it or not, she was going with it.

"I like the middle one," she eventually said. She knew she could have run next door, asked Candy or Amelia for their opinions. Candy would of course be all too happy to speak her mind. But Amelia was busy, and Amelia had her own business and paint colors to think about. Or not. She made those decisions quickly and didn't second guess any of them.

Trust your gut, she thought, remembering Amelia's advice.

Cole nodded once. "Good."

"What is that supposed to mean?" she asked, sliding a glance at him.

His mouth quirked a little as he walked over to a stack of paint cans she hadn't even noticed when she'd arrived. He picked one up. "Because I took a gamble and loaded up on these this morning. Figured I'd get a start on it while I wait for the rest of the supplies to arrive."

She shook her head, but she couldn't help but laugh. "And what would you have done if I'd chosen another shade of yellow?"

He popped the lid on the can with a tool from his pocket. "I knew you wouldn't."

She narrowed her eyes, not quite sure if she was annoyed with his confidence or just surprised by it. The boy she'd known growing up had been broody and sullen and a loner.

But then, maybe she hadn't really known him at all. She'd just observed the side of him that he let people see.

"You have good taste," he finished, and she blinked at him in surprise, more flattered than she probably should be.

"Oh." She ran her tongue over her lips to hide the thrill of such a compliment. "Thank you."

"What's with the box?" he asked, motioning to the dishes.

She picked it up, deciding to move it to the small storage closet in the back for safe keeping. There was a lot going on in this bakery and she'd be better off keeping the dishes unpacked until she was closer to her opening, she realized. The dust alone would make washing them now pointless. One more thing that she hadn't thought of initially. All part of the learning curve, she supposed. "These are the dishes for the bakery."

She didn't know why she felt the desire to show some of what she'd found, but she unwrapped a tea cup anyway and showed it to him. It was one of her favorites: robin's egg blue with sweet little yellow and white butterflies painted in a whimsical pattern around the edge.

"My mother had china from her grandmother that she always brought out for special occasions. I wouldn't want to use that here, of course, but it made me think of collecting pieces at antique shops around the area."

"So none of them match?"

Maddie carefully rewrapped the cup and set it back in the box. "Nope. Each piece is different. That way you never know which one you'll get. Each visit to the bakery is its own sort of surprise."

She could imagine Robbie's little girl Keira liking that.

"Interesting," Cole said with a funny look.

Maddie bristled as she closed the lid. "Interesting? I don't know if that's a compliment or not."

"Just an observation," he replied.

Maddie bit back a sigh. The man was impossible to read, and not exactly willing to reveal his inner thoughts. She thought back to that silent, scowling boy at the bus stop, who had simply walked away when she extended a moment of kindness.

Some things didn't change.

Deciding not to let his lack of enthusiasm for her idea

ruin hers for it, Maddie collected the box and carried it out to her car, breathing in the breeze coming off the lake as she slammed her trunk closed. There was a chill in the air and she pulled a sweater from the backseat. It would be sweater season soon. She could almost imagine the people from town sitting at tables that lined her window, looking out over the lake, while the warm smell of cinnamon rolls filled the air.

She smiled to herself as she walked back inside.

She had planned to tell Cole that she would check back later, but the truth was that her afternoon was free. The appliances had been ordered. The cabinets and other supplies, too. And now, thanks to Cole, the paint color had been selected.

The light fixtures were already ordered and set to arrive any day now. She still had to order the furniture, and get a help wanted ad written up for the paper. But she didn't feel ready to commit to either of those items on her task list right now. She was stalling. But she was also strangely drawn to the man who was spending nearly as much time in her new establishment as she was. Who was putting just as much effort into bringing it to life.

She walked back into the shop, where Cole was hunched beside the paint cans. A slip of brown hair had fallen over his forehead, shielding his eyes.

"Anything I can do to help?" she asked, expecting him to gruffly dismiss her, tell her that he had it all under control.

To her surprise, he said, "You know how to paint?"

She nearly laughed, recalling the time that she and

Cora had begged their father to let them repaint their rooms, and Maddie had stepped on an upturned paint can lid and tracked marks all over the wooden floors of her bedroom, which she'd then frantically scrubbed for hours until every last bit of evidence was gone.

"I'm not very good at it."

He slid her a glance, showing he wasn't convinced.

"I mean it," she said, lest he think she was trying to get out of something. "I'm sort of…clumsy."

"Well, you're going to need to get over that once you're running your own business," Cole said. He picked up a brush and stood, facing her, his hand extended, waiting for her to step toward him. "You can do the trim. Tape's in the toolbox."

"I actually have a bunch of pies to make for the market on Sunday," she said, knowing that this was a pretty bad excuse, and an outright lie, considering she always baked those pies on Saturday afternoon and Sunday morning.

"The market is forty-eight hours from now," he said, and for some reason, she was surprised that he was even aware of her family's market, or that he knew when it was, even if it was a major weekly event in Blue Harbor. "You telling me you sell stale pies? Something tells me that sort of thing won't work once you get this place up and running."

Despite herself, she couldn't refrain from grinning. Begrudgingly, she stepped forward, her fingers skimming his when she reached for the brush, and a bolt of excitement shot through her. His skin was warm, even smooth.

And his eyes were deep and unwavering when they locked on hers.

She swallowed hard and backed away. Now wasn't the time to be getting sidetracked. Maddie held the brush in her hand and considered Cole's words. It was true, that owning her own business meant that she'd have to do more than just bake in the kitchen as she'd done at the café. She'd have to step out of her comfort zone, deal with all sorts of business issues that she'd never even considered before.

She pushed back another burst of panic as she picked up a can and got to work.

*

By Saturday afternoon, the entire bakery had been transformed into a warm, sunshine yellow, not that she could thank herself for it. After seeing just how poor of a painter she was, Cole had banished her from the premises for the day—not that she would have come anyway. She had pies to bake for the market tomorrow, and an extra one for her book club meeting this evening. The brownies that she was still trying to get just right in time for her opening were cut into thick squares; Maddie had tasted the batter but not the final product, and she hoped that they turned out moister than the last time she'd experimented with the recipe.

Now, she set the bakery boxes down on the folding table, noticing that in addition to the walls being finished, the space had been cleaned up. Cole had swept. And put away all his paint supplies. The entire space felt clean and bright.

Maddie stood in the room, taking in the fresh color, as the reality of it all took hold. It was no longer the stationery store. It was her bakery, with its fresh yellow walls. Soon it would have chairs and tables and a counter filled with her creations.

She pulled in a breath, realizing that it was shaky. As much as she had longed for this and wished for it and thought that she was ready for it, now she couldn't stop thinking of just how much it was. Work. Money. Time.

Amelia made it look so effortless, even though Maddie knew firsthand just how hard she worked. Still, she had it figured out. When a problem arose, she didn't panic; she simply solved it and moved on. She knew her busy hours, and she knew her customers' favorites. She knew how much of which ingredients to order without having to worry about getting it wrong. What if Maddie ran out of sugar the first week? What if she had more customers than she could tend to and ran out of everything before the day was half over?

What if she had no customers at all?

She closed her eyes and pressed her fingers to her temple. She couldn't think about any more of this. She was supposed to be stopping by, to see how things were progressing, not stand here once again wondering if she had made the biggest mistake of her life.

She locked the door behind her and hurried up the gravel path to Main Street, training her eye on the bookshop in the distance. It was run by Bella Clark—Gabby's cousin on her mother's side—and Maddie passed it daily but didn't have a chance to drop in as often as she would have liked.

The sky was overcast and there was a threat of rain in the air as she approached the storefront, which boasted a flowerbox full of golden orange mums at the base of its wide, bay window. There was a display set up of mysteries—something that seemed fitting for the season—and already Maddie could see that the room was filled with women from the town, all of whom she knew, of course. That was small-town life for you. A few new people came in, like Candy, but otherwise, it was family or friends that you'd grown up with all your life.

And guys that you'd grown up with, she thought, considering the lack of new faces in Blue Harbor.

Still, for some reason, she wasn't thinking of the possibility of new faces. She was thinking of an old face. One she'd grown up with, but maybe never properly looked at before.

Ridiculous. She shook away any strange sort of fond thoughts of Cole and pushed through the paned front door on which hung a quaint little sign. Maddie made a mental note to look for something similar for her own door—something that wasn't just functional, but showed that she took pride in the small details. And Bella definitely took pride in that.

Inside the room was warm and smelled of autumn-scented candles. The lamps on the end tables gave an inviting glow and a circle of mix-matched chairs had been arranged near the back of the room. On another table, wine and coffee were set up. Maddie set down her offerings and helped herself to a glass of red wine.

"Oh, this smells good," Gabby said as she bent down

to smell the pie. Noticing the brownies, she said, "And you did bring these!"

"I do know how to bake more than just pies," Maddie joked. Her cinnamon rolls were a big seller, and she had an arsenal of cookie and cake recipes, too. Still, part of having her own establishment was the perk of experimenting with new recipes and flavors. She'd always loved spending her free time creating new ideas, but now she had a purpose.

"Well, these won't last long," Gabby said. "And for sure you'll be invited back."

Maddie grinned, happy that she had taken Gabby up on the offer to attend the meeting tonight. She glanced around the room, noticing Bella talking to the town librarian, Helena. Over in the corner was Gabby's youngest sister Jenna chatting with Mila, who ran an art studio not too far from town. Her long, red hair was always a giveaway, and Maddie had longed for such a unique feature when she was younger. Something to set her apart. Or make her feel special.

Growing up as the youngest of four sisters, she often didn't just feel like she was living in their old clothes, but also following in their premade footsteps. It was easier that way, but as she grew older, she yearned for something of her own.

She just hadn't realized how difficult it would be to have it.

"You're frowning," Gabby pointed out.

Maddie startled. She forced a little smile. "Was I? Sorry, just looking out for Candy."

"Candy must be over at the café, right?" Gabby asked, and Maddie felt a wave of nostalgia bloom. Of course. It was still a busy time of year for Blue Harbor. Tourism was usually steady through October. With the summer help gone, Amelia would of course need Candy's help to pull off a Saturday evening service. She wondered if she should have volunteered…until she remembered that Amelia had all but banished her from the café within days of Matt approving the building permit.

Clearly, Amelia was aware of Maddie's doubts. Or maybe she just knew that it would be so tempting for Maddie to go back to the tried and true path. The one her sisters had already walked on and carved out. The one that was safe.

"Besides," Gabby said, giving her a little grin. "Candy likes to take her books out of the library. And then forget to return them."

Maddie laughed at this. "I seem to recall that Amelia paid her late fee last month." It was a kind gesture, and she knew that Amelia was starting to see the good in their father's girlfriend, as Britt had done too—and that was shocking. Of all of them, Britt had been the most protective of their mother, the most hurt by her loss. Candy had been a surprise to her, and not a welcome one.

But then Candy had won them over the way she had their father. Maddie thought back to her father's words, insisting that Candy just wanted to help, and be included.

And then she thought of the way Candy had helped. Sly. Very sly.

But still. Cole was working out; Maddie couldn't deny

that, not she was entirely ready to forgive Candy. Yet. The last thing she needed was the woman thinking it was okay to meddle when it so was not okay.

Gabby motioned to Bella, who had come to the refreshment table. "I brought a newcomer."

"So I see!" Bella smiled warmly. She was in Amelia's grade, and at this age, two or three years rarely made a difference, yet somehow, it did. Like Maddie's sisters and cousins, Bella had her own business, this lovely little bookstore that she'd transformed over the years, from a dusty old space into a charming place on Main Street. Her window displays were always fresh. She was ambitious with her events—finding local authors for readings, hosting this book club, and story hours for children. She even had a poetry circle and a writing workshop once a month. She was forever hanging up a new poster, and her store was always busy, yet never cramped.

Maddie hadn't made time to read lately, she realized. "Once I get the bakery up and running, I need to stop in here more often."

Bella just tipped her head and took a sip of her drink. White wine for her. "How's it coming? I saw Cole's truck down near the lakefront earlier today, loaded with supplies."

Maddie felt her heart skip at the mention of his name, though she wasn't sure why. "He's my contractor," she said, as much as it was a reminder to herself. He was a contractor. He worked for her. Though oddly, she was starting to feel like he was running the show.

"So he said," Bella said. Then, perhaps seeing the confusion on her face, Bella added, "He stopped in here yesterday. He usually does on Fridays."

Maddie stared at Bella as her mind processed this information. "Cole comes to the bookstore?"

Bella shrugged. "Once a week, sometimes more. In fact, I stock the mystery section just for him. Though lately, he's been buying more romance."

Maddie felt her eyes bulge as she glanced at Gabby, who looked equally stunned. "*Romance*?"

"For his mother." Bella laughed. "Sweet, huh?"

Sweet wasn't the word that most people in town associated with Cole, but Maddie didn't comment on that. She was beginning to realize that there was more to Cole than he'd let on. Or that people saw.

Bella glanced at the brass clock on the wall and sighed. "Looks like we should grab a seat. Honestly, it will be good to sit down. But first, I might need one of these brownies."

Maddie held her breath as Bella took a small bite, waiting for a knit of the brow, a small frown, or a polite gesture that she was too full to finish. Maybe she'd put in too much sugar, or not enough. Chocolate could be bitter without the right ratio.

Bella's eyes lit up as she took another, larger bite. "There's only one problem with you opening a bakery, Maddie."

"What's that?" Maddie nearly whispered. Her heart was beating so loudly, she was nearly sure that Gabby could hear it beside her.

"I'll need to double my daily squats to make up for all the extra calories I'm going to consume!"

Maddie felt herself visibly relax. It was silly, she knew. She knew how to bake. She had done it every day, for years, long before her mother was gone.

But those were her mother's recipes. Like Amelia's café or the orchard, it was safe. Established. And tonight's offering was something entirely her own.

She added a brownie to her plate and took her seat, in between Gabby and Jenna, and smiled at Mila across the way.

They began discussing the book that Maddie had only skimmed, but even if she had read it in its entirety, Maddie knew that she wouldn't have been able to contribute to the conversation right now. Her mind was on something else.

Or rather, someone else.

Cole came in here once a week. Bella seemed to think nothing of it. And Cole bought romance novels. For his mother.

Bella was right. That was sweet. Even sweeter than her brownies tonight, she thought, taking a large bite.

6

The market was busy for a fall weekend, and Maddie sold out of her pies within the first hour. She regretted not saving one for her father, but she also knew that she wouldn't have a chance to see him tonight, even though she tried to pop over whenever she could on Sunday evenings—pig roast or not. But today there was too much to do with plans for the bakery, and she still had the Harvest Fest to prepare and shop for, too. She knew how many ingredients she needed on hand for her pies each week, but the festival would be much bigger, with higher demand.

Good practice for the opening of her bakery, she told herself.

She spotted Britt across the converted barn that had housed the market for years and held up a hand to get her attention. She usually stuck around on Sundays to help where she could, but today she needed to get going. Cole wasn't scheduled to work, so there would be no development on the construction since yesterday, but she hoped to get a start on the week.

Besides, she reminded herself…it was one thing to continue to help her family's various businesses. Now she had her own to think about.

"Do you mind if I head out today?" Maddie asked when Britt finally made her way over to her. "I'm hoping to get a few more items crossed off my list."

"How's the bakery coming along?" Britt asked, and from the gleam in her eye, Maddie knew immediately that she'd been tipped off about Cole. "I hear Candy hired you a mighty fine contractor."

"Very funny," Maddie said drily. "Actually, it's coming along better than I expected."

Britt frowned. "What do you mean? Do you have doubts about the new business?"

Maddie hesitated. She knew that Britt would be more than happy to share her thoughts on how to make the bakery a success; she'd done wonders with the orchard in the brief time since she'd taken over the daily operations from their father.

But something was stopping her. She wasn't sure what would be worse…admitting that she was in over her head or having Britt point out that the choices she'd already made were not the right ones.

There was no going back on some of those things now. All she could do was forge ahead.

"Oh, you know how little hiccups can arise when it comes to construction work," she said casually, wishing that she hadn't even hinted at her concerns.

Britt nodded knowingly. "Oh, yeah. You have to keep an eye on Cole. You remember what he was like as a kid!"

Maddie pinched her lips. She felt oddly defensive of Cole, and she didn't like where this conversation was headed.

"He's been really helpful, actually. It's…surprising."

Britt looked unconvinced. "Huh. Well, I guess people change and grow up. So you think the work will be done on time?"

"I hope," Maddie said, and then, upon seeing the pinch of Britt's brow she said, "I mean, of course. Actually, I think Cole may be ahead of schedule."

"Wow!" Again, Maddie had the sense that Britt wasn't buying into what Maddie was saying, or maybe, she could see through to Maddie's doubts. Or maybe, she knew what she was talking about, and her experience had taught her to be a little more guarded. "Well, I'm excited to see what you do with the place."

Maddie pulled in a breath and released it. "I hope you like it," she said, and at that moment she realized just how much Britt's approval meant to her. Nearly as much as Amelia's, but that couldn't be topped.

"Maddie, given the success you have with the pies each week, I am sure the bakery will be just as successful," Britt said, and Maddie didn't know whether to smile or cry.

She'd mastered her mother's pie recipe. She could turn out a dozen or so pies once a week for the market. She could assist Amelia in her expertly run kitchen.

But taking it all to a whole new level? All on her own?

That was unchartered territory.

*

She decided to walk home again, but Gabby was just climbing into her delivery truck when Maddie emerged from the barn. She rolled down the window and stuck her head out. "You sold out quick today!"

"Apple pies are usually a big hit," Maddie said. She would have made more, but she hated to have extra, even though she knew that her family members would gladly take them off her hands. "I've been thinking of ways to incorporate seasonal flavors onto my new menu. What do you think about apple turnovers?"

"Yes, please!" Gabby grinned, and Maddie made a mental note to highlight that item on her list. "Maybe a crisp, too?"

Maddie considered this. She felt her spirits buoy at the conversation. "I could make them individual-sized," she thought aloud. Yes, crisps were easy, and who didn't love that buttery, sweet topping on a cold, fall day? "I could warm them up for each order."

"All this talk of food has me hungry," Gabby said. "Care to grab a bite in town?"

"At the café?" It didn't close until after lunch, and Maddie wouldn't mind seeing Amelia. She missed her daily routine. Craved it, really. Life had been so much more secure when she knew exactly what she had to do each day, without having to give it much thought.

Gabby wrinkled her nose. "I was thinking we could go to the pub. It's livelier. Besides, I really don't think I could deal with Candy on my day off. Could you?"

Maddie laughed. Gabby had a good point, and the pub was livelier. And it wasn't next door to her bakery either. Or a reminder of everything she'd given up.

"Okay, then." She had work to do, but the day was

wide open, and besides, Gabby was good for her. Gave her ideas, and let them flow without force. Calmed her down a bit too.

"Thanks for the lift," she said to her cousin. Once again, the feeling of depending on the strong women around her left her unsettled. She reminded herself that she lived in a town where whatever you couldn't walk to, you could bike to, mostly. The orchard was on the edge of town, but it wasn't a place she visited more than once a week. And she needed to stretch her budget. Focus on what was really needed. Like the tables and chairs for the café.

She made a mental note to place the order by tomorrow, no matter how much she waffled with her decision between clean lines and classic, old-school charm. Amelia's café was more eclectic; Maddie had never seen Amelia fret over the chairs not matching the tables, or the artwork all being different, and mostly from local artists. Each item she added to her café was something she liked. A part of her.

Maddie reminded herself that just as the café had come together, so would the bakery. She just had to go with her gut. Like Amelia said.

There were several restaurants and bars in Blue Harbor—it came with being a resort town and the ferry port for the charming Evening Island not far off in the lake. But the Conway girls had long ago adopted the pub at the Carriage House Inn as their favorite spot, and it went without saying that Harrison's, while popular with the men in town, was off-limits after Gabby's sister Brooke married Kyle Harrison years back, and shortly thereafter divorced him and left town.

The pub was busy when they arrived. Jackson was tending bar, and he waved to them when they walked in, deciding on a spot at the bar today, rather than a secluded table. It didn't need to be said that Gabby was holding out hope that a tall, dark, handsome stranger would saunter in, slide onto the stool next to her, and basically propose marriage by the time the sun set.

She was a hopeless romantic. Really, she read too many novels for her own good.

Maddie's stomach grumbled as she studied the menu, but she knew she needed energy if she was going to get through the rest of the day.

"I'll have a coffee and the scrambled eggs," she said to Jackson, ordering from the weekly brunch menu.

"Well, you're no fun!" Gabby chided. She grinned at Jackson. "I'll have a Bloody Mary."

He winked at her and Maddie stifled a sigh. She doubted there was anything more than banter and flirtation stirring between those two, but she still envied the way they both pulled it off with such ease. She couldn't remember the last time she'd flirted. Or dated.

Really, she had no time for such a thing anymore. She now understood why Amelia had been so determined to stay single.

Except that Amelia wasn't single anymore, was she? She was back together with Matt.

And there he was, Maddie noticed, perking up.

"Hey, Matt!" she called out as he approached the bar.

Noticing them, he seemed to relax and came over to the empty chair beside Gabby.

Gabby's lips pinched only slightly that a man who was spoken for had taken the seat that she was clearly holding out hope for. Maddie knew her so well.

"Amelia meeting you here?" Maddie asked as she glanced at the oversized, vintage clock on the wall.

"I'm meeting her later on," Matt replied. "Thought I'd kill a little time until she was finished up for the day."

"You coming to Harvest Fest next weekend?" Gabby asked, and Matt laughed.

"As if I have a choice? Amelia has me helping out. I'm almost expecting a detailed spreadsheet of my duties." He looked pleased at the thought of it. "I wouldn't miss it."

"Family tradition," Maddie mused. When she was younger, they all looked so forward to the big day at their orchard, when the grapes were harvested for wine and the entire town seemed to come out to help with the effort. Her mother would make pies and the girls would hand out cider for refreshments, to thank everyone for pulling together. Over time it had grown into a larger event, and Maddie knew that Britt had big plans for this year.

"I'm helping with the decorations," Gabby said.

"And I'll be selling baked goods, of course," Maddie said. She already knew the mini pies would be a hit, and the opportunity to give the townsfolk an early preview of some other treats she'd be offering at the bakery was something she intended to take full advantage of.

"I'm surprised you find the time with the bakery opening so soon," Matt remarked. He managed to keep a straight face when he said, "Amelia told me about Candy's part in everything."

Maddie rolled her eyes. "Actually, it all worked out, not that I'll be letting Candy off the hook just yet."

"You admit that to Cole yet?" Matt asked. He jutted his chin toward the other end of the bar. "There's your chance."

Maddie sat up a little straighter as her heart sped up. Cole was here? In the pub? She supposed it wasn't completely out of the realm of possibility. He'd been here before, alone at the bar, talking to no one, sipping his drink and then leaving silently. But back then he'd just been someone from town. Now…

Well, now he was starting to feel like a part of her life.

She looked down the length of the bar. Sure enough, there at the far end, hunched over a beer, his eyes on the game on the television screen, was Cole. Normally, she wouldn't have even considered drawing his attention or interrupting his solitude, but now it was impossible not to. What was she supposed to do? Ignore him? The man might like his space, but it didn't feel right.

She stared his way, hoping to draw his attention, and finally caught his eye. She gave a little smile and a wave, and she felt Gabby nudge her hard as Cole's mouth lifted into a slow grin and he slid off his stool, drink in hand.

Maddie shifted over to the seat that had opened beside her, but not before Gabby hissed, "And you said he was just your contractor…"

Maddie narrowed her gaze at her but composed herself before Cole caught on.

"We were just talking about you," Matt told him as Cole slid onto the seat in between Gabby and Maddie.

Immediately, Maddie was aware of his presence. She could feel the heat of his skin and sense the size of him, so much larger than Gabby, who was no bigger than a wisp. She stole a glance at the muscles that pulled against his long-sleeved tee shirt. Her cheeks flushed when she caught Gabby watching her do so, her smile rueful.

"Oh boy," Cole said, sliding Maddie a rueful smile. "That's rarely good."

Maddie relaxed into her chair, enjoying the banter. "Tell me about it. I might have to actually let Candy off the hook at this rate," she said, sparking a laugh from Gabby.

"Something tells me that Candy has something in mind other than your bakery being finished," her cousin replied, giving a suggestive lift of the brow.

Maddie felt her cheeks flush and she quickly said, "So, Cole, you never told me where you learned to do what you do."

Cole's jaw tightened as he shifted his gaze to stare at his glass of beer. His shoulders hunched as he took a long sip. "Just things you learn along the way."

Maddie knew all about learning along the way; she had no formal culinary training after all, and neither did Amelia. But they had their mother. The best teacher of them all.

"Oh, but someone must have shown you the ropes?"

Cole went quiet for an unnerving amount of time and kept his eyes trained on the television. "Can't really credit anyone."

Gabby exchanged a glance with Maddie. Right. Time to change the subject.

"Well, I can't wait for it to open. I'll be the first in line. Jenna, too," Gabby said.

"Maddie said the bakery is coming along quickly," Matt continued.

"Your plans make it easy," Cole said gruffly. It was true that Matt's plans were clear and concise, and detailed the design of the space exactly to Maddie's vision. With his support and expertise, she at least knew that the layout of the space would be fully functional and beautiful. "I was going to head over there later and start opening up that wall—get a head start on tomorrow."

Matt glanced at his watch. "Amelia should be wrapping up soon. I can walk with you if you'd like."

Maddie wasn't sure what surprised her more. That Cole seemed receptive to socializing with Matt, or that she was suddenly disappointed at the thought of Cole leaving so soon…even if it was to work on her bakery. What he was hired to do. What she should care most about right now.

Cole's phone vibrated on the table. He looked down at the message that had just come in and frowned. "Change of plans," he said, grabbing his coat from the back of his chair. "Looks like I won't be in tomorrow, after all."

Maddie sat up in a panic. All those warm and strange feelings were immediately replaced with the same old feeling she always had when she thought of Cole. Disappointment. Only this time it was personal.

"What do you mean, you won't be in? Tomorrow is

the only day to cut the doorway through the cafe," she reminded him. "It's the only day of the week that Firefly is closed. I promised Amelia we wouldn't disrupt her business. And I'm on a time frame."

"The job will be done on time," Cole grunted. He glanced at his phone once more before shoving the device in his pocket. "But I won't be in tomorrow."

"But—" But he was gone. Turned and walked out the door before she could even form her protest. The words left hanging in the air much the way her bakery now felt.

Would he be finished in time? Or be back at all? She hadn't paid him yet, but that didn't necessarily mean anything.

"Did I say something to upset him?" Maddie asked Gabby, who looked just as confused as Maddie felt.

"Didn't his father own that construction company?" her cousin asked.

Maddie chewed her lip. Regardless of what Cole's father did or didn't do, or where Cole learned his skills, one thing was clear: Cole was still unwilling to open up. And she should have known better than to try.

After all, he'd just up and bailed on her.

He was still the same exact person he was all those years ago.

*

Cole arrived home in seven minutes, but it felt like seven hours. Traffic in Blue Harbor was always at its peak on the weekends, with tourists cruising down Main Street, or driving through to check out the scenery. Most of them probably thought it was too cold to walk or bike today, even though the leaves were nearing peak foliage. He supposed that the wind was sharp, but it didn't stop him from cursing under his breath when he finally pulled into his driveway and killed the ignition. The cans of paint he'd purchased for the exterior of the house sat in a neat pile to the side of the garage, a bitter reminder that time was fleeting and that there was still so much to do.

Janice opened the door before Cole had time to fish out his key. Her eyes were wide with alarm, but her shoulders seemed to relax with relief at the sight of him.

"She's sleeping now, but that was scary, Cole. Never saw her like that. Suddenly so pale and weak. Between you and me, I think she's in more pain than she's letting on."

Cole's jaw tensed. Of course, his mother was in more pain than she was letting on. That was just like her, always trying to be strong, for him. Couldn't she see that it was his turn now, to be strong for her?

Didn't she know that despite all her efforts, ever since he was a kid, he'd seen right through the brave smile to the hurt that lingered in her eyes? That he'd carried that pain inside him, helplessly, until he was old enough to do something about it.

Yet here he was, thirty years old, and there was still not a damn thing that he could do.

He clenched a fist at his side, wanting to punch a wall or kick something over. To release this frustration that was building inside him without release.

But that was something he'd done as a kid. Kicked

rocks. Punched trees. Gone down to the lake and screamed out over the water, letting the waves carry away all his pain.

He wasn't that kid anymore.

And he was going to do something to help her if it was the last thing he ever did.

"Call the hospital and let them know we're coming," he told Janice, who immediately winced.

"She said she didn't want to—"

He was already halfway up the stairs. He didn't pause. "Call them. Please."

The insistence must have gotten through to Janice because he heard her mutter something under her breath as she picked up the house phone and dialed the hospital— she didn't need to be told which one. It would be a thirty-minute drive but he'd get there faster than it would take an ambulance to get here and back.

He found his mother in her bedroom, on top of the worn patchwork quilt that had been there as far back as he could remember, covered by a green knitted blanket that he knew Janice had brought over as a gift around Christmas. The curtains were drawn, and the bit of light that peeked through the fabric lent shadows on the wall.

His mother was so frail he could lift her in his arms like a child. And that's what he did before she could protest.

"Cole. It's no use," she said.

He didn't answer as he carried her down the stairs, past the worried lines that etched Janice's face as she stood near the door, wringing her hands, and out to the truck, which was still warm.

"We have to try, Mom," he said as he started the engine and backed the truck out again.

He had to try.

7

On Tuesday morning, Maddie was woken by the ringing of the phone. The sun was barely peeping through her curtains and one glance at the clock told her what she already knew. It could only be Amelia, who would have been at the café for over an hour by now, and awake well before that.

Someday soon Maddie would be back on that schedule. Amelia must have forgotten that for now, Maddie had no reason to get up so early. She'd purposefully made the cinnamon rolls last night so that all she needed to do was hand them off to Amelia—in an hour and a half.

So much for catching up on rest.

She hadn't been sleeping well for too many weeks now, and something told her that she wouldn't return to blissful, dream-filled nights of slumber once the bakery opened and she had even more things to worry about into the quiet hours of the night.

"I thought when we were doing laundry yesterday that you said Cole wasn't going to be working yesterday," Amelia said by way of hello.

Maddie frowned and rubbed the sleep from her eyes. She took a minute to adjust the pillows behind her back so she was sitting up in bed. She'd stopped by the bakery yesterday afternoon before she'd placed the order for the tables and chairs, so she could measure for the hundredth time, triple-check her decision to have twelve tables in total, some which would seat two, others four. She'd decided on round, bistro-style tables, in a rich walnut stain that matched the floors, with lighter weight cross-back chairs that would be easy to move about the room.

She must have been there for an hour. Probably more like two, because she was so nervous about hitting "send" on her purchase agreement.

Cole had never arrived, not that she'd been looking for him. He'd made his intentions clear on Sunday.

"He wasn't working yesterday," she confirmed. But something in Amelia's tone, in the entire reason for her calling at all, told Maddie that this was not true. Her heart began to pound with panic. She couldn't afford for anything to go wrong right now. Not with her tight budget or her hopes to open in two weeks. "Why? What are you trying to say?"

She could hear the amusement in her sister's voice when she said, "Well, I'm standing here, in my café, looking straight into your bakery."

Now Maddie tossed the quilt from her legs and scrambled toward the closet. "What are you saying? Cole knocked through the wall?"

"Oh, he more than knocked through it," Amelia said. Maddie could practically picture her sister shaking her head. "I'm not complaining, but you said he wasn't working, so I'm a little surprised."

"Let me get ready," Maddie said. "I'll be there in fifteen minutes."

She disconnected the call and flung open her chest of

drawers, reaching for her favorite pair of jeans and a long-sleeved tee. A shower could wait. She needed to see exactly what Cole had done—because Firefly Café was open for business all day every day until midday Sunday, and no more work could be done on that doorway until then.

She should be grateful that her sister took things in stride a little more easily than she did.

Maddie was at the café in twelve minutes, the two trays of cinnamon rolls she'd prepped last night stacked in her arms, ready to slide into Amelia's oven. The café wasn't open to the public yet, but despite the sign on the door, Maddie knew it was unlocked. She entered and let her eyes pull her to the part of the wall that was supposed to come down. To be an open doorway joining the two establishments.

A large clear tarp was tacked to the wall. Maddie held her breath as Amelia poked her head through the open window pass that led to her kitchen and disappeared again, only to swing through the kitchen door a moment later with a funny expression on her face.

"How bad is it?" Maddie asked, nervously, as she handed over the trays. It was one thing to get everything wrong with her bakery. It was another to mess up anything for Amelia. After everything her sister had done for her over the years, the last thing she would ever want to do was sabotage this café, even for a day.

Amelia set the trays on the counter. "Pull back the tarp and see for yourself."

Maddie walked to the tarp and, like a band-aid, ripped it back. She gasped. She wasn't quite sure what she'd expected to find. A haphazard hole. Exposed wires. A work in progress.

Instead, she was looking at a framed doorway. The trim had already been painted. Amelia's walls were touched up. She was looking right into her bakery, past the wall of windows that fronted the porch.

"But this…This must have taken all night."

"I'd think so. And yet you'd never even know that anyone was here." Amelia gestured to the floor and her counters. "Not a trace of sawdust. It barely even smells like paint. He must have cracked the window."

Maddie didn't even know what to say. She shook her head and let the tarp fall back into place, shielding her unfinished bakery from Amelia's customers.

"He told me he wasn't coming in yesterday," she said again, trying to wrap her head around his change of plans, and why he'd failed to inform her. He'd known she was annoyed. She'd been pretty clear about that. Either he'd done the work overnight as a peace offering, or because he was a man of his word.

Or maybe, a bit of both. Whichever way she looked at it, she couldn't deny the feeling that Cole was turning out to be a different man than she'd expected. And that she was a little more pleased by this than she probably should be.

"Guess he never specified last night," Amelia said with a little grin.

"He did say the job would be finished on time," Maddie said slowly, recalling his words, how hard she had been on him. How tense things had been when he'd left.

Looked like once again Cole was a man of his word. And she owed him an apology. For a couple of things.

*

Cole pulled his truck to a stop outside the bakery and reached for his thermos of coffee, only to realize he'd already drunk every last drop. He'd need another cup to keep him going, and Firefly Café should probably be just opening its doors by now. He could use the opportunity to ask Amelia how she felt about the doorway, and if she needed any touch-ups to the work.

He walked around the porch to Amelia's side of the building and up the steps to the front door. Inside the café, it was warm and sweet-smelling. There was already a buzz in the air. Most tables were full, and the counter stools were occupied by locals he recognized. He'd expected to see Amelia standing near the display case, but instead, his eyes hooked on Candy. Or rather, hers hooked on his.

Her entire expression lit up and she nearly poured a pot of coffee all over her own hand. As it was, she sloshed the hot liquid all over the counter rather than into the ceramic mug she held. With a laugh at herself, she apologized to the waiting customer, handed over the coffee, and called out to him as she wiped up the mess.

"Yoohoo! Cole!"

Despite the hellish thirty-six hours he'd just had, Cole felt a smile pull at his lips. Unlike the rest of the people in this town, Candy didn't know his history. And it showed.

"Hello, Candy."

"You here for my famous cheese biscuits?" If he didn't know better, he might say she had just batted her eyes at him.

He was flattered, and maybe even more flattered that she had her sights set on him for Maddie, but she was focused on the wrong guy. The only thing he could ever bring Maddie, or any woman for that matter, was disappointment.

He'd learned more than how to change a light fixture from his father, after all.

He set his thermos on the counter. "Here for a coffee, actually."

Candy gave him a little wink as she topped him off and then added two cheese biscuits to a white paper bakery bag. "On the house. I'm sure you have another big day at the bakery ahead of you. Unless you want to sit and chat for a bit? I'm sure I could get one of these gentlemen to slide down and make some room for you at the counter." She gave him a long look.

Given the fact that these gentlemen were aging locals who were only on page one of the daily newspaper, or bent over in thought on today's crossword puzzle, Cole doubted this very much. But then, taking another glance at Candy, he supposed that she was quite a convincing woman. After all, she'd gone well out of her way to ensure that he took the job at the bakery.

And why was that exactly, he wondered now.

He considered asking her but doubted she would give him a straight answer. Besides, it was plain as day, wasn't it? She was trying to set him up, just like his mother and Janice next door.

Really, would his life be that much better if he had someone to share it with?

He pushed back that thought, knowing the answer as much as he'd tried to deny it all his life. Getting close to people was a risky business. It was better, in the long run, to keep them away.

Even someone as sweet as Maddie Conway.

Only the older he got, the harder it was to adhere to this way of thought. And the more time he spent with Maddie…

He shook his head, deciding to keep things professional. He knew, however, that Candy wouldn't make that easy for him.

"I'm sure Maddie won't want me sitting around talking when I could be getting work done," he said with a grin.

"Pfft," Candy said, brushing a hand through the air. She gave him a conspiratorial wink and leaned far over the counter. He had the instinct to back up, but he didn't want to hurt her feelings. She was a nice lady. Warm, if a bit overbearing.

"That Maddie has a heart of gold," Candy said. "A hard worker, too. And talented! Have you tasted her cinnamon rolls yet?"

Knowing he probably had no choice but to humor Candy, Cole let out a low whistle and considered this question. "Can't say that I have," he said.

"Well, you're too late for any today. Those things sell out in minutes." Candy raised an eyebrow.

"Is that so?" Cole remarked.

Candy nodded. "Oh, yes. And you know what they say, don't you, hon?"

Cole wondered if he stayed silent if she would stop talking. He could only assume whatever he said or didn't say wouldn't change the outcome of this conversation.

"A way to a man's heart is through his stomach," she said, giving him a sage look. "That girl will have half the men in town in love with her by the end of the opening weekend of that bakery. Mark my words."

Cole rubbed a hand over his mouth to hide its smile. "Very interesting, Candy. I'll certainly have to try one of those cinnamon rolls one of these days."

"I'll set one aside for you first chance I get," Candy said.

"Well, as for today, thank you for the biscuits, Candy. I'm sure I'll enjoy them."

"Homemade. By yours truly!" She winked again.

"You'll be stiff competition for Maddie, then," he said as he sipped his coffee. A line was forming behind him, he noticed, but Candy didn't seem to let this bother her.

"Oh, no, this is a family effort. We all support each other. Have each other's best interest at heart." She smiled. "But then, I'm sure you understand. I hear that you and your mother are very close."

The old, younger, angrier Cole would have stiffened at this. Asked why she knew this and who she'd learned it from. But eventually, he'd come to realize that no one really heeded him as much attention as he thought they did. That really, no one thought of him at all, and that it was easier to fade into the background than he'd ever realized. Sure, it had been a hot topic for the gossip circle when his dad had upped and left, but that was twenty years ago. It was old news. And people in a small town like this… They lived for fresh gossip.

Candy, he could tell, liked to be in the know.

"That we are," he said, pushing back the tightness in his chest when he thought of his mother, home now, after spending Sunday night in the hospital, only to be released the next day with new pain meds and little else. There was nothing to be done, really, was what they were telling him. They tried to prepare him, tried to explain what he should expect, but he hadn't wanted to listen, stormed off, told himself it couldn't be true.

At that moment, the angry child had reappeared. The scared child, he supposed.

It was another promise he'd made, so many years ago. To never be afraid again. To never feel loss. To never put himself in the position of feeling that kind of pain, or fear losing someone he loved.

To never love again.

"Well," he said, jutting his chin to the wall with the tarp. It wasn't exactly the sightliest scene, but until the bakery was ready, it couldn't exactly be unveiled. "I was hoping to see if Amelia liked the doorway."

"Oh, we were most impressed!" Candy exclaimed.

"We?" Cole asked.

"Maddie and Amelia were marveling over it all morning!" Candy gave him a long, suggestive look. "I can tell that Maddie is most impressed."

Cole wasn't so sure about that, but he decided to let the comment pass. "If Amelia needs any changes, she knows where to find me."

"I'll let her know. She's busy back in the kitchen now."

Cole nodded. He reached into the bag and pulled out a cheese biscuit. Took a big bite that put the rumbling in his stomach at bay.

Candy watched him expectantly. He grinned back at her. "Good. Really good."

"Oh, you flatter me so," she said, giggling loudly.

Cole chuckled to himself as he let the next customer step up to the counter and walked back to the door. He was flattering her because he'd never really been a biscuit-loving person. But he'd made her smile.

And given what Candy had done for him, finding him the job, and giving him a chance, he supposed it was the least he could do.

*

Maddie was pretending to look over her itemized project lists when Cole came to the door. Even though she'd kept one eye trained on it since watching him pull up and then disappear into the café next door, she still jumped when she saw him.

His expression was impossible to read as he stepped inside, holding a thermos in one hand and a bakery bag from the café in the other.

"Good morning." His tone was even, belaying no hard feelings about how they'd left things on Sunday, and no apology either.

It was obvious that he didn't plan to offer up an excuse for his absence. Or try to get credit for the work he'd done either.

"Good morning," she replied. She set down her papers and motioned to the tarp hanging from the doorway. "You've been busy, it seems."

Cole gave a modest shrug and took a sip from his thermos. "I said I'd get the project finished on time, and when I make a promise, I stick to it."

She nodded, narrowing her eyes on him. Interesting. "Thank you. It looks wonderful, and Amelia thinks so too."

Cole shifted his gaze, grumbled something under his breath, and then, when the silence grew too heavy, held up the bakery bag. "Biscuit? Compliments of Candy."

Maddie grinned at this. The work was separate; Cole had made that much clear. But this was his way of extending a peace offering.

Or an apology.

She'd take both. But not the biscuit.

She wrinkled her nose. "I'm surprised that Amelia lets her sell those things."

Cole reached into the bag and pulled one out. He took a big, hearty bite, chewing thoughtfully. "They're good. I like them."

"Well, I don't," Maddie said, crossing her arms. She was aware that she sounded like a child, and she could see the gleam appear in Cole's dark, hooded eyes. She watched him pull the last of the small, fragrant biscuits from the bag, suppressing a sigh. "Candy's just...well, it's a lot at once. First, she becomes part of the family." Not in the legal sense, but Maddie wouldn't be surprised if it eventually came to that, God help her. "And now she's at the café. She took over my position."

"But didn't you have to leave the position to start your own business?" Cole pointed out.

"Yes, but…Well, I did. I wanted a change. But…some days I think that I preferred things the way they used to be."

Cole nodded slowly, as if he completely understood, even though she wasn't sure she understood it herself. She couldn't have both worlds. You couldn't move on with your life if you were rooted in the past.

Or maybe, she thought, as her gaze drifted back to her stack of papers and the list of items for her menu, you could. Right there, at the top of the list were her favorite recipes, passed down from her mother.

"Well, with the open door, you still have one foot in the café, right?" Cole polished off the last bite of the biscuit and flashed her a wicked grin. "And Candy mentioned your cinnamon rolls this morning."

Maddie frowned. There was no telling what Candy had been feeding him all morning. More than biscuits, that much was for sure. More like a heavy helping of gossip.

"Of course, she also let me know they were all sold out. In fact, she implied that every man in town is in line for them each morning."

Maddie felt her cheeks flush with heat, and she started to protest, but really, how did you combat Candy's nonsense?

But Cole just laughed and set down his thermos. "Before I get back to finishing the kitchen, where did you want the sign when it arrives? Over the door or along the long wall outside?"

"The sign?" Oh no, she had completely blanked. Her heart drummed inside her chest as it pulled the blood away from her face. "I...I completely forgot."

How could she have forgotten? It was right here, on her list! And how could she even think of opening a bakery without a sign? She was supposed to place that order by yesterday morning to ensure it arrived in time. Instead, she'd gotten sidetracked by her conversation at the pub on Sunday and planning for the Harvest Fest this weekend.

"I could put a call into a shop I know," Cole offered. "They're pretty quick. What's the name going to be?"

"Buttercream Bakery," she said, wondering how he would react to that. She had filled two notebooks with ideas for the name before finally settling on her choice. She had considered asking Amelia her opinion, but she was almost afraid to hear her sister suggest something different when nothing else seemed to stick.

"I like that," Cole said with a grin, and for reasons that Maddie couldn't explain, she felt her shoulders sag in relief.

Really, she told herself, as she picked up her pen and went back to her notes, determined to not forget anything today. What did it matter if her contractor thought she'd picked a nice name for the shop?

But from the smile that stretched over her face, she realized that it did matter. Because Cole was turning out to be more than a contractor.

He was starting to feel like a friend.

8

Maddie stood in her brand-new kitchen, running her hand over the smooth marble counters, and tracing her fingers over the shiny new appliances, thinking how different it looked, just days earlier. Now, complete as requested by Friday, it was exactly as she had envisioned it. It was light, airy, and above all things, functional. It was perfect.

And she almost couldn't bear the thought of actually putting it to use.

Cole emerged behind her, making her jump, and she turned with a hand on her chest to see him standing in the doorway, giving her a funny look. "Are you just going to stand there gaping at it?"

"It's amazing, Cole, really," she breathed.

She thought she saw a little pink rise up in his cheeks, but he averted his gaze and firmed his mouth. "I'll be starting the installation on the bakery counter today. Might be noisy."

"I'll be baking today, so I probably won't leave the kitchen," she told him. Tomorrow was the Harvest Fest, and she had pies and mini pies, and muffins and turnovers to crank out before she closed up shop for tonight. She was thankful for once that the Sunday market was canceled in light of the busy weekend. Usually, it was something she looked forward to each week. And despite all the extra work, she didn't intend to give it up. That orchard was her family business, and she was still a part of that family, even if she had a bakery to run.

She'd find a way.

Somehow.

Cole nodded once before disappearing into the main room, letting the brand-new swing door to the kitchen fall closed behind him. Maddie felt giddy as it did so; she hadn't even noticed that earlier when it had been propped open upon her arrival.

Now Maddie stood in the middle of the room, alone, left to completely take it in. Her kitchen. Alls hers. Just the thought of it filled her with nervous excitement. This was really happening.

Only none of it would really happen if she let the entire town down at the Harvest Fest tomorrow, would it?

Right. It was time to get to work. She had lugged flour and sugar and other dry ingredients over to the bakery throughout the week, carrying as much as her bicycle basket or hands would allow, and she transferred everything from the main room to the kitchen, her last bags being the two she'd carried over today: the butter and cream and other perishables that she now loaded into her beautiful new refrigerator. She took time to organize everything so it would be within easy reach, and she couldn't wait for her new canisters to arrive so that she would have her main ingredients within easy reach. For now, though, she would have to deal with the large bags she had stacked in her new pantry. Cole had maximized the space by adding a rack on the inside panel of the door.

Another feature she hadn't asked for or thought of, but which would be extremely useful.

Should she be annoyed that he was taking liberties, or grateful that he'd been so thoughtful? She decided on the latter and decided to thank him the first chance she had. She knew better than to interrupt him when he was using a power tool.

She went to the storage room for the largest of the bags of flour and sugar—and hesitated when she saw her mother's apron, folded in tissue paper on the top shelf, beside the stacks of plates. She hesitated, and then before she could give it any more thought, she reached for her trusty blue and white striped apron, issued to her on her first day over at the café, and looped it over her neck.

Her mother's apron was threadbare and soft, a hallmark of sweet moments spent in the kitchen of their big home, baking pies for the market with Maddie's assistance. It hung on a hook for years after she was gone, and Britt had been understandably upset to see Candy wearing it one time. Maddie was just happy she had been spared the sight. But even though Britt wanted her to have it, Maddie wasn't so sure she had earned the right.

Why not Amelia? Amelia with her successful café?

Maddie worked through her list, starting with the dough, which she let chill while she peeled apples. She had five hundred hand pies to get through, and thanks to the four ovens, she was able to get through nearly a hundred with each batch. But it didn't stop there. There were the muffins, too. And the large sheets of apple crumb cake that she'd serve in slices.

She baked without stopping until the counters were full of cooling hand pies that would then be transferred to the bakery boxes she'd ordered in bulk. She hadn't even realized how much time had passed, until Cole appeared in the doorway, his tool case strapped over his shoulder.

"Breaking for lunch?" she asked, kicking herself for letting her eyes drop down over his hard, wide chest.

He gave her a slow grin. "Breaking for the day, actually. You haven't stopped, and I didn't want to interrupt you."

"Wow." Maddie set down the wooden spoon she was using to toss apple slices with brown sugar and cinnamon. "I guess I lost track of time."

"You know," said Cole as he looked at the white cardboard boxes she had stacked and assembled in the corner of the kitchen. "Now that you have your own bakery, you could put a label on these."

Maddie considered this long enough to realize that he was completely right and that yet again, she'd had an oversight.

"It's too late now," she said, glancing at the clock on the wall. It was past four. She still had to make pie dough, filling for another sixty hand pies, and never mind the muffins. She'd saved the easiest item on her list for last, but it didn't mean that it wouldn't take time. "I have too much to do."

"I could help," Cole offered.

She hesitated and then shook her head. "What about the counter?"

"I'm waiting on the glass now for the display case. Won't be in until Monday."

She glanced at him. It was Friday, and it was nearly the end of the day. And she didn't want to take advantage of his kindness. But she couldn't swing the rest of her prep work for the festival and get the labels printed, too.

"If you're sure. I'll pay you for your time."

He cut a hand through the air. "Nonsense. Happy to help. You have the logo?"

She did. She'd paid a freelancer to design it a few weeks back, locking in her decision for the bakery name. And yes, she did lose sleep that night, considering what a big step that had been.

"I have the file on my phone," she said, pulling the device from her back pocket.

He handed her a business card with his contact information. She wasn't sure why she was surprised to see that he had one. Maybe because this was Blue Harbor, where everyone knew everyone.

Or maybe because she hadn't exactly considered getting any cards made for herself.

"Send me the file and I'll get it over to the printers. You should probably get some business cards made up while you're there. And maybe something for the window? Something to let people know exactly when you'll open? Create a bit of a buzz?"

She marveled at him, wondering just who this man in front of her was. Not the one she'd known growing up, that was for sure.

"I can't believe I never thought of this," she said, wincing.

"You're busy with other things," he said, gesturing to the rolling pin that was sitting in a pool of flour.

She shook her head, feeling her cheeks heat. "But it's like you said the other day. I can't just hide back here and bake all day. This is my business. I'm in charge of a lot more than pie crusts now." She felt hot tears burn the backs of her eyes and she willed them not to fall.

It would be one thing to let Cole see her cry. It would be another to get the pie dough all salty.

She picked up the rolling pin and turned her back slightly to him, so he couldn't see her struggling to compose herself.

"True," Cole said lightheartedly, "but for now I think your main priority is pie crusts."

She glanced at him over her shoulder, surprised to see the kindness in his eyes as he gave her a smile.

Just as quickly, it fell, and he nodded once. "I'll head over to the print shop now. Send me the file while I'm on my way."

She watched him go, back through the door, leaving her alone in the kitchen again. And despite the fact that she still had hours of baking ahead of her and hadn't stopped for lunch, and her brand-new, beautiful pristine kitchen was now an absolute mess of flour and mixing bowls and berries and open canisters, the entire bakery smelled sweet and felt warm and inviting and…hopeful.

*

Cole took the liberty of filling in the information for the business card. Normally, he'd see this as overstepping, and if Maddie saw it that way, he'd offer to pay for the cards. They weren't much, and the teenage boy behind the desk offered to put them together while he waited. Said it was the most business they'd had all day.

"It leaves plenty of time for homework," he said with a shrug.

Cole figured the boy was roughly seventeen or eighteen. A junior or senior in high school, most likely. "Staying around here for college?" he asked while the kid uploaded the file and stood by the machine, waiting for it to process.

At this, the boy's otherwise bored expression came to life. "Got a full ride to Northwestern."

Cole nodded at this. "Impressive."

"Yeah. I've never been to Chicago. Never really been anywhere."

Cole gave him a little smile. "Me either," he admitted.

"Really?" The kid didn't look like he believed that. "But you're…No offense, sir, but aren't you like…thirty?"

In other words, an old man, at least according to this kid. Cole laughed, despite the inadvertent insult, realizing just how much life experience could be gleaned in twelve or thirteen years. How much someone could grow. Or change.

But he'd never been like this kid. Never had a scholarship to a high-profile college or any college at all. Never even applied to college.

He'd lived in this town all his life, but like this kid, he wasn't going to stay here forever.

And with his mother's health declining by the day, it wouldn't be long now before he was gone for good.

The kid collected the stack of business cards and held them out for approval. Cole studied the card, at the swirly logo that Maddie had created, and her name below it. She hadn't specified what color she'd wanted, but he'd taken a gamble and gone with a shade of purple that popped and complemented the buttery yellow that was now the hall-mark color of her bakery.

"Looks great," he said.

"Are these for like, your girlfriend or something?" the boy asked as he put the labels and printed information sheet in a bag, along with the box of business cards.

"A friend," Cole said, shutting down anything more than that immediately.

But it wasn't an excuse, he realized. Maddie had start-ed to feel like a friend. The first he'd had in Blue Harbor in a long time. If ever.

*

Maddie was rolling out the last of the pie crusts when Cole returned, an hour later. She brushed a strand of hair from her forehead with the back of her hand and looked down at her apron, now coated in flour.

A good reason not to wear her mother's apron, she told herself. But not the main reason. No, that cut much deeper.

Cole set the bag he was holding down on the only clear space of countertop to be found and walked over to the island where she stood. He leaned down, smelling the pies that were cooling on one end, and gave her a look that showed he was impressed. "These smell amazing."

"Please, take one, for your troubles," she said distractedly. Only she wasn't distracted by the work she still had to do tonight or the fact that she'd chastised herself for the better part of an hour over the labels. Really! What right did she have to be going into business when she was overlooking the most obvious facets of the business?

But no. Now she was distracted by the shadow of stubble that graced Cole's jaw line, and by the way the corners of his eyes crinkled when he grinned.

He shook his head. "Nah, you save these for tomorrow. I can tell you've been working hard."

Not hard enough, Maddie thought. Baking was only part of the job, and she couldn't let the management end of things slide away.

She glanced up to give him a little smile, but her heart skipped a beat when her eyes locked with his and didn't shift away. He was staring at her, with that intense look she had come to accept, or even like, and he was leaning slowly across the counter, closing the distance between their bodies. Her breath locked in her chest when she considered what must be happening. That he might have been picking up on the same things she had.

Instead, his hand went up, and she felt the warmth of his skin brushing at her face.

"You had flour on your nose," he said, showing her his thumb.

"Oh," she breathed, smiling foolishly. "Oh." Of course! Of course that was all it was! Honestly, what did she think the man was going to do? Try and kiss her?

And if he had?

She pursed her lips. No sense in even thinking about that.

"I brought you these," he said, opening the bag on the counter to reveal sheets of labels that were so perfect, and so absolutely beautiful, she gasped out loud. "And I didn't know exactly how you wanted the business cards, but I took the liberty. If you don't like them, I can have them redo them. They weren't very busy today."

Maddie studied the card, her chest swelling with pride when she saw her name in a clear font, the name "proprietor" underneath.

"It's perfect," she said.

"And I also brought you this," he said, reaching into the bag and pulling out a premade salad she recognized from the grocery store. Clearly, the poor man wasn't up for another ambush by Candy over at the café. "I took a wild guess that you probably won't stop for dinner."

"Is this all part of the job description?" she asked, giving him a grateful smile.

He shrugged that away, his eyes skirting around the room. "Happy to hear there aren't any complaints about the kitchen."

"Nope," Maddie said. "I've certainly put it to use, too." She laughed at the mess, knowing that she would have it all cleaned up before she left for the night. Whenever that was.

The thought of a long night and even longer day tomorrow made her weary. "Tomorrow will be a big day. I had thought I might have staff hired to help out, but it didn't make sense to bring someone on the payroll until the bakery is days away from opening." She'd train them, get them up to speed. Even if she just started with one person, working the counter and helping with prep, she could handle the baking on her own if need be while she assessed her daily demand.

That was the plan at least. But things didn't always go to plan when it came to running a business, she'd realized.

"I could help out tomorrow," Cole surprised her by saying.

She almost wasn't sure she had heard him correctly, and she watched him, waiting for him to take it back, or clarify. Instead, he just gave a casual grin. "Not part of the service. Just...an offer."

Her heart was hammering in her chest and she knew she was grinning broadly. Too broadly. But she couldn't help it.

"Only if you're sure. I mean...yes, please! But...it's a long day," she warned.

"I've got time," he said.

"Thank you," Maddie said. "Thank you!"

Cole's eyes hooded as he attempted to hide his smile, but she could tell he was pleased as he mumbled his parting words and headed out for the night.

Maddie turned back to the messy kitchen, from the bakery boxes to the cooling treats, to the salad that she would now eat for energy.

She'd come into this kitchen today feeling alone, and a bit overwhelmed. But now, she had backup. Even support. Someone who was as vested as she was in making this place a success.

Someone who cared.

Question was, did he just care about the bakery, or was there more to it than that?

9

Maddie didn't know why she had bothered to put on lipstick. Or leave her hair down when a ponytail or braid
would have been so much more practical. Or why she had
worn her good knee-high chestnut brown leather boots
that were typically reserved for nights out with the girls,
rather than the work boots that would have been the obvious choice for standing outside on a farm on a chilly fall
day.

But of course she knew, deep down, why she had
done it. She just hoped that no one else picked up on it,
too.

No such luck, she soon realized. She stifled a sigh as
she stood behind the stand where she had just finished
stacking her pie boxes, and saw Cora tilt her head from a
few yards away, where she had been helping Britt set up
the pony rides for the children. That was a new addition
this year, and Maddie suspected it had a lot to do with
Robbie's daughter Keira.

"You're all dressed up!" Cora said suggestively as she
sauntered over to where Maddie stood.

Maddie darted her eyes around the Harvest Fest, wishing Cora would keep her voice down, and hoping that no
one else had overheard. Cole hadn't arrived yet, and she

was still trying to push back the worry that he might not come at all.

Only this time she wasn't concerned about him not keeping his word.

No, this time she was concerned he might have a change of heart.

"Am I?" Maddie feigned innocence. "It's what I usually wear this time of year."

"For a night out!" Cora narrowed her eyes in suspicion as her lips suppressed a smile. "Hoping to find an eligible guy at the Harvest Fest, huh?"

Maddie felt her shoulders relax. She knew as well as Cora that there would be no chance of that, at least not seriously. Sure, there might be a tourist in town for the fall weekend, but usually, the only guys coming to Blue Harbor for the fall activities were family men, already married, or dragged along by their girlfriends for some "country air." The summer was the real chance for a fling—and nothing more. You couldn't exactly form a relationship with someone who wasn't going to be staying in town, could you?

Still, Maddie decided it was best to go with this theory. Throw Cora off the track. Candy and Gabby might be open to the idea of giving Cole a second chance, but her sisters still harbored the same view that was the general consensus here in town. That Cole was broody, moody, and unpleasant.

Except that he was turning out to be none of those things.

"You caught me," Maddie said. "Guilty as charged."

She smiled as she began stacking paper plates and napkins.

"Well, I give you credit for trying," Cora said with a sigh. She looked down at her own attire, sadly. Jeans, a flannel shirt, and a vest for added warmth. Her auburn hair was pulled back in a low ponytail. Her feet tucked into weather-appropriate wellies to avoid all the muck. "Britt has me signed on to help with the children's section today. My best shot at finding romance is a single dad."

"Or a fun-loving uncle?" Maddie tried, but they both knew it was pointless. It was fall, winter would come sooner than they expected, and with any luck, they'd both be far too busy with their businesses to even have time to think about finding men.

Except that now, as Maddie watched over Cora's shoulder as Cole approached, men seemed to be the only thing on her mind. Or rather, one man in particular. A man who had surprised her, and who was here to support her. Out of the kindness of his heart or out of charity, she wasn't sure.

Or maybe, she thought, with a quickening of her heart, out of interest.

He was looking around, meandering through the gathering crowd, and she held up a hand and waved when their eyes met.

Cora, looking at this exchange with confusion that quickly morphed into interest, widened her eyes, speaking a thousand questions without saying anything at all. Maddie pretended not to notice so she didn't have to feed into it. Really, she should have expected this would happen.

After all, there was no telling how Candy would react when she saw Cole was here.

"Cole, you know my sister, Cora, right?" Maddie felt a little breathless and resisted the urge to smooth down her hair. That was another thing she hadn't counted on today: wind. The gusts were going to blow the napkins clear across the orchard to the apple trees if she didn't weigh them down.

Cora shook his hand, raking her eyes over him, still not saying anything.

"Haven't seen you around in a while," she eventually said.

"I don't get out much," Cole said gamely.

That wasn't exactly true, Maddie was quickly learning, but still, Cole was a bit of a loner, always sitting by himself, never with a friend.

Which was why it was particularly interesting that he had volunteered to spend the day here today.

Don't read too much into it, Maddie, she scolded herself. Maybe, she realized with sadness as she thought back on her childhood, the reason he always sat alone was because no one invited him over. Certain routines and habits eventually stuck.

"Cole's going to be helping me with the stand," Maddie explained. Then, seeing the shock in her sister's face, she added, "You know that Cole is doing the work on the bakery, right?"

Cora just nodded. Very, very slowly. Finally, with wide, unblinking eyes, she began to back away. "Well, I should probably get back to my station. Cole, nice seeing you. Maddie, we'll talk later?"

Even though it was framed as a question, Maddie knew that there would be no escaping an interrogation. She pursed her lips and managed not to roll her eyes. The last thing she needed was to sit around discussing her contractor with her sister as if…as if something was going on between them.

Obviously, nothing was. Except…

She stiffened as Cole brushed against her hip, her arm. She hadn't factored in how tight the space would be, or how long the day would last. She couldn't exactly move to the side without getting her leather boots dirty by a puddle of mud from last night's rainfall. And even though she was wearing her best cashmere sweater (she'd forgotten that, though clearly, Cora had noticed) and omitted a jacket, she felt the heat coming off Cole's body, warming her.

"Thanks again for helping," she said, giving him a smile.

Something passed through his eyes that she couldn't quite read. And lingered. Instead of shifting his gaze as he had done so many times, he left it there, trained on her, the faintest hint of a smile forming the corner of his lips.

"So this is what the locals do for fun around here," he finally said, looking out over the crowd.

She laughed. "You mean, you never came to Harvest Fest?"

But then, she'd been to every Harvest Fest, obviously, and she had never seen him. He didn't come to any town events, not as a kid, and certainly not as an adult. Did he want to? She wondered now if he'd felt left out. If she should have tried harder to be his friend back when they were young and he was still her neighbor.

"Not really my scene," he said, and then, perhaps catching her frown, he said, "But now I see that I've been missing out."

"On town festivals?" she laughed. Few single men in town bothered with them.

His eyes seemed to lock onto hers and hold them there. "On a lot of things."

Right. Maddie licked her lower lip and quickly looked away, her heart beating so loudly inside her chest that she was near-certain that Cole could hear it. She needed to keep busy, at least until the festival filled up, and then she expected she'd be too busy to even worry about the fact that Cole was standing so close to her that she felt more like a couple than a team, and that she liked it. A lot.

Nervously, she started explaining the pricing and told him how many of each item she had made. She was just getting through an overly detailed description of the muffins when she spotted Candy out of the corner of her eye, coming directly toward them.

Maddie groaned under her breath. "Brace yourself. Here comes Candy."

She didn't have enough time to see Cole's reaction. Candy was already on them, her eyes round, her smile huge.

"Well, isn't this a picture!" she exclaimed, giving a dramatic wink in Maddie's direction.

Maddie kept her face expressionless. She would not feed into this. She would not argue. She would turn the conversation back on Candy. It was her only hope.

"Helping out with Amelia today?" It had, after all, been Maddie's job in the past. Together they'd plan and prep for every festival, working side by side in the kitchen of the café and then schlepping over the containers of food to the festival destination. They had a routine, one that was well-rehearsed and ran smoothly, and even though it was still always a little stressful, Maddie longed for those long days with her sister.

Sure, she was just a few yards away, but it wasn't exactly the same. The ride over had felt like a taste of the past, when they'd loaded the trunk of Amelia's SUV until they didn't think they could fit any more. It was the same for every festival, only this time they were working separate stands.

"Oh, a little of this, a little of that!" Candy wiggled her shoulders. "Your father insisted on overseeing the harvesting crews, and with his arm and leg all healed by now, I couldn't exactly protest."

Maddie turned to Cole and explained, "Candy was my father's caretaker, after his accident."

Cole raised an eyebrow. "Accident? I didn't know, I'm sorry."

"Oh, he fell off a ladder." Maddie shook her head. She and her sisters were unanimous in their opinion that their father never should have climbed so high, all on his own. And Maddie knew what her mother would have had to say about that, too.

"Boys being boys." Candy grinned fondly, and then looked at Maddie with a sense of camaraderie.

Maddie said nothing. She really wished that someone

would come along and buy a muffin, and not just because she was worried about having too much on hand.

Candy seemed to take her cue, saying, "Well, I don't want to interrupt. And I really should go help Amelia, even though she did ask me to check on your father…"

Maddie suppressed a grin. She knew from experience just how busy Amelia would be setting up for the day, and if she was already sending Candy off under the pretense of checking on their father, she must really need a break.

"Why don't you go check on my dad," Maddie said, "and I'll see if Amelia needs a hand. I'm already set up here, and Cole can watch the stand for a few minutes."

She glanced up at him to see if that was okay, but she realized with a start that she had known it would be. And that she rather liked that.

That somehow, over the past week and a half, they'd become something of a team.

Maddie walked over to where Amelia stood, her cheeks flushed despite the chill in the air, and a look of fury in her eyes when she spotted Maddie. She glanced around quickly before whispering loudly, "She is driving me crazy!"

"You're the one who hired her!" Maddie couldn't resist. She started to laugh.

"Only because you decided to open your own bakery," Amelia grumbled.

"Last I checked you all but kicked me out your kitchen door. I could have helped longer," she pointed out. And she'd tried, and offered, but Amelia had been insistent.

Amelia shook her head firmly now once again. "No.

122

You never would have gotten things going at the bakery if you were still helping me out every day."

Maddie knew this was true. Standing on her feet all day at the café was tiring, and time-consuming, and getting the bakery ready for opening day was proving to be a bigger undertaking than she'd expected.

"It is a lot of work," she admitted.

"You can handle it," Amelia gave her a reassuring smile. Her first of the day. "And Cole is doing a great job, so Candy says." She raised an eyebrow. "I see he's here today. You didn't mention that on the way over."

"Nothing to mention. He's just helping me," Maddie stated pertly.

Amelia just lifted her eyebrows. "If that's what you're calling it."

"Now you sound like Candy!" Maddie would have swatted her sister if she'd been standing any closer.

"What can I say? I spend too much time with the woman." Amelia began laughing and handed Maddie a stack of paper plates. Without explanation, Maddie knew just what to do. For a moment, it felt like old times again.

"There," she said when she was finished, and Candy could be seen making her way back.

"We still have our groove," Amelia said brightly.

Maddie nodded a little sadly. They did. And she missed it. And she wasn't sure if she would ever find it again all on her own.

Only looking over at the stand where Cole was standing, assisting a mother and her two young children to three apple muffins, Maddie thought that for today at least, she already had.

*

The day was long but went by quickly, with constant activity at the stand making it impossible to spend much time trying to chat with Cole or let her eyes linger too long on those deep-set eyes, which had a way of pulling her in and keeping her there.

By the time she closed up shop, it was deep into the afternoon. The festival was still going on, with pony rides and face painting for the children, and Cora was now helping to distribute cider while Candy hovered near Amelia, who was getting ready to help feed the dinner crowd. Soon the strings of lights would come on and the sun would set and the music would pick up, and even Britt might sit down on a hay bale and relax for a bit. For now, though, there was more work to be done.

"Thanks for helping today," Maddie told Cole. "I'm honestly not sure that I would have been able to handle it all on my own."

"Sure you would have!" Cole helped her box up the last of the napkins and bakery bags. "But I was happy to be here. Fresh air. A change of scenery. All good."

She gave him a small smile, hesitating as she contemplated whether she should ask him to stay. She opened her mouth to speak at the same time he did, and laughed. "You first."

"No, ladies first. I insist."

She swallowed hard, losing her nerve. "I was just thinking that maybe I should hand these leftover items to Amelia, in case she needs them. She might need my help."

Although, if recent history proved anything, Amelia would be more inclined to shoo her away.

"What were you going to say?"

He looked a little bashful as he pushed his hands into his pockets. "I was going to see if you wanted to give me the grand tour. But I can see you're busy. Another time."

Maddie immediately regretted not saying what she meant earlier and straightened her back, hoping the eagerness didn't show too much in her face. "I can never resist showing off the orchard. Besides, Amelia will just tell me she doesn't need my help, even when she probably does."

"She sounds a lot like you then," Cole commented, and Maddie paused for a moment. It was true that despite probably needing her help or an extra set of hands, Amelia was determined to handle everything without the one person most willing to pitch in.

She supposed they were both self-reliant like that. Or stubborn. Two traits they had inherited from their parents.

Or maybe, they were just always putting each other before themselves.

"You know, you're right. I never thought of it like that. And...I'll take it as a compliment. Amelia is my greatest inspiration. Well, other than my mother, of course."

She glanced over her shoulder as they began walking to see if any of her sisters or cousins had noticed her slipping away, but the festival was still crowded and lively. It felt good to disappear into the quiet fields after such a chaotic event.

She closed her eyes and breathed in the sweet, fresh

smell as the sounds faded behind her. "I love it here," she said, opening her eyes to find him looking at her closely. She felt her cheeks burn. "Sorry, I always love the clean air, and the quiet. This place is as much my home as the big house on Water Street."

She led him through to the apple orchard, which was mostly picked over by now. "You know," she said, laughing, "when my sisters and I were little, we'd meet our cousins here and play an epic game of hide and seek while our parents worked."

Cole grinned. "Did you always win?"

"Of course!" Maddie grinned. "But Britt was so competitive; she put up a good fight, even if she was the oldest."

"That must have been wild, growing up with such a big family."

"It was." Maddie laughed, thinking of the few times that a fight would break out, usually over something as trivial as who had last misplaced the hairbrush. "Sometimes I don't know how my father handled it all, once it was just him."

But she did know. Because of Amelia. It was Amelia who cooked their dinners and made sure that she and Cora had everything they needed for school. And it was Amelia who made sure she properly cleaned her skinned knees when she fell off her bike. Who gave them the female role model that they needed. Who didn't fall apart.

Now, just like then, Amelia took things in stride.

"You had each other," Cole remarked. "I'm sure he was grateful for it."

"Sure, and my aunt and uncle helped a lot too," Maddie said. She slowed her pace, her heart growing a little heavy as it always did when she thought back on that time.

Eventually, Cole filled the silence. "I always wanted a big family as a kid."

This was the first insight he'd given to his past, and she waited to see if he'd elaborate. He didn't. "And now?"

Cole shrugged. "Might be nice to have family."

"At least your mother is close. Besides, it's not always easy having so many family members," Maddie said slowly, as her anxiety began to pick up again as she stood at the edge of the field and looked back over the neat rows of trees. "Especially when they're all older than you and more established, and well, more successful."

"You're successful," Cole pointed out. "You're the youngest of the group and you're starting your own bakery."

"Yes, but..." She wanted to say, but would it be a success? Would people come? Would they like what she made? Would she make it through the slow months, before the summer people returned?

Instead, she just shrugged. "I guess when you always have someone telling you what to do or carving a path, or just...making things easier for you, it's hard to think about doing something all on your own."

"You could ask them for help?"

Maddie shook her head. "That would defeat the purpose. Besides, they're busy. I don't want to be a burden. I want...I guess I want to make them proud. I want to show them that thanks to everything they showed me and gave me all these years, I could apply that towards something, you know?"

Cole nodded. "I feel that way too, sometimes. But family…well, family just wants what's best for you."

Maddie slipped him a sidelong glance and smiled. "You're very wise, you know."

"I do know, actually," he replied, dead-pan, before his mouth quirked into a slow grin that made her heart flip over.

She was so busy staring at it that she tripped over an abandoned basket that they distributed for apple picking and lost her footing, lunging forward, until she felt a strong, firm hand on her arm that righted her quickly.

"You okay there?" They were standing face to face now, and in the golden hour of waning sunlight, she could see the softness of his eyes that crinkled at the corners when he smiled.

"I'm okay," she said, a little breathlessly.

His hand was still on her arm, warm and strong, and his gaze was so intense that she didn't think she could tear her eyes away if she tried. Her heart was beating so loudly, she was sure that he could hear it, and she wasn't so sure that she could blame it on her stumble.

Cole's gaze dropped to her mouth, and ever so slowly, he leaned in. Maddie pulled in a breath, her heart positively pounding now, and started to close her eyes.

But Cole dropped her arm and cleared his throat, and jutted his chin over to the barn. "Candy's over there."

"What?" Maddie's eyes flicked right to the woman doing a poor job of spying from behind the red barn. Her big blond curls were a dead giveaway.

Cole let out a laugh, low and steady, and despite what could have been an awkward moment—that was now lost—she joined him.

"I should probably get going anyway," he said.

Maddie wanted to encourage him to stay, to join in the rest of the festival activities, but she decided not to press. The man had almost kissed her. She needed some time to think about that.

"Well, I'll, uh…see you Monday. At the bakery."

She nodded, swallowing back the things she wanted to say, the urge to reach out, hold his arm, just a little bit longer.

"See you then," she said, giving him a little wave as he walked toward the parking lot and she made her way back to the festival. "And thanks."

"It was my pleasure," he replied.

No, Maddie thought, sucking in a breath that went straight to her giddy heart. It was hers.

10

Maddie awoke the next morning to the sun filtering through her linen curtains, the heater pushing out warmth, and a sense of hope that she hadn't felt in a very long time, not even when she'd worked up the nerve to open her own bakery.

Without even stepping outside, she knew that it was the perfect fall day. Sunny and crisp outside, and warm and cozy inside. Growing up, these kinds of days had been her favorite, marked by the start of school, and a sense of anticipation for a new year and all that was to come. It was also the kind of day where she enjoyed helping her mother in the kitchen after school or on weekends, with the sunlight pouring in through the windows, and the kitchen so warm and comforting and smelling so rich and inviting that she could truly understand the meaning of the word home.

Without needing to give it much consideration, Maddie decided to bake. There was no market at the orchard today, because of the ongoing harvesting activities that were separate from the festival. The staff would be occupied pressing the grapes, preparing them for the wine. And she always dropped off a double batch of cinnamon rolls on Saturday for Amelia, so that Sundays she didn't have to worry about it.

Technically, she had a day off. But baking was in her blood, it was what she did.

It was who she was.

Her recipe box was in the small kitchen of her apartment, on the little shelf over the range. It was a modest kitchen, even vintage by today's standards, and certainly nowhere near as sleek as the gorgeous one she now had at the bakery, but this was her home, and while the kitchen was small, it was familiar and wonderful and she loved every inch of it, from the painted, Shaker-style cabinets, to the butcher board counters, to the little timer that was shaped like a rooster that had been with her for so long that she didn't even remember when or how it had first come into her possession. But she could guess. One of her sisters had given it to her, for Christmas or her birthday. Most of her most cherished possessions were given to her by her sisters. But their wisdom…that was really the greatest gift of all.

They'd imparted so much. Shared so much. And now it was her turn to show that it had not all been in vain. That she had been listening, watching, admiring. And respecting.

She tied on her home apron (a gift from Cora three years ago, even though it was covered in a print of gingerbread men holding candy canes) took a mixing bowl from the cabinet over the range, and reached for her canisters. Many happy times had been spent in this small room, trying new recipes, or just enjoying the routine of following one of her mother's tried and true recipes. This kitchen was also where she did her own taste testing, mixing ingredients and jotting down notes, dreaming up new ideas, and then watching, and waiting, and seeing if they were as good as she had hoped or needed tweaking.

Today she wasn't going to bother with any experiments. She was going to make one of her favorite recipes from childhood—one that her mother used to make with her on those first days of fall. It was an apple cider cookie, something she planned to offer at the bakery, but today she wasn't making it for any customers. Today, she was making something for Cole.

As a thank you. To show her gratitude. After all, he had not only done amazing work at the bakery, and helped with her business cards and labels, and come to the Harvest Fest yesterday, but he'd also challenged her, listened to her, and made her almost feel less alone in this daunting process.

And of course, there was the fact that he'd almost kissed her.

And as Candy always liked to point out, there was a sure way to a man's heart...

Her own heart skipped a beat as she measured out the flour. Even though she had the recipe card in front of her, she didn't really need to refer to it. There were some things that were just ingrained in you, a part of you, and this cookie, and the memories it held, was one of those.

She worked the batter up quickly while the oven preheated and then slid the cookie sheets into the oven, careful to set the timer. She used the time to shower and dress, and when she emerged back into the kitchen with seconds to spare, she smiled at the scent. Yes, it was officially fall. Harvest weekend. Apple cider cookies.

What could top that?

She could think of one thing…

She pulled the cookies from the oven and carefully set each one on the wire cooling rack. By her estimation, she had just enough time to dry her hair…and apply a little lipstick. With that finished, she boxed up her cookies, slid her feet into her best leather boots, grabbed her favorite soft and wooly scarf, and checked her reflection in the mirror near her door for good measure.

The leaves rustled as she walked through town, toward Cole's house. If he wasn't home she would just stop by her father's house instead. He'd be happy for the cookies, and by her calculation, Candy should be safely tucked away at the café by now. It might be nice to have a little one-on-one time with her dad, she mused. Maybe, that's really how she should be spending the day.

But that was the chicken's way out, wasn't it? And she'd been taking the easy path for far too long. She hadn't come this far without seeing it all through. The bakery.

And her heart.

Cole's house was near the cross street, whereas her own childhood home was right on the waterfront. His home was also smaller, but then, few families in town were as large as the Conways. Growing up, the McCarthy house had been the house to avoid. With shame she remembered that she and her sisters used to skip it on Halloween, afraid of a prank that Cole might play, or other years, when there was no light on, welcoming children to ring the bell.

But it was a sweet house, charming really, and Maddie looked at it with new appreciation. She could see now that there were rose bushes and hydrangea shrubs and even a window box nearest the front door. The summer flowers had long lost their bloom, but there were mums under the small awning and curtains pulled from the upstairs windows. Had these little touches always been there?

Back when they were kids, this house had felt sad, and neglected, and made them quicken their pace as they pedaled by it. Now, she saw that the front door had a wreath hanging from a metal hook, and there was a charming red mailbox hung beside it.

She knew that Cole had worked on the house in recent years, but had it always looked this way, she wondered? Or had something changed?

But she knew the answer to that deep down. Something had changed. And it was something inside her.

With a big breath for courage, she walked purposefully to the front door and knocked three times. When no one answered, her heart rate eventually resumed normal speed as she considered what to do. Perhaps Cole was around the back, enjoying this beautiful day on the patio or tending to the yard?

She glanced at the driveway, where his truck was parked. Surely, he was home.

She was still deciding between whether knocking again was bordering on stalker territory or just giving up and walking away when there was a turning of the locks and the door swung open.

Maddie dropped her gaze in surprise to see Cole's mother standing in the hallway. She hadn't seen Mrs. McCarthy in…years, she realized. Like Cole, his mother rarely came into town, and never frequented the café. There were rumors, of course…about a troubled marriage, about money problems. Everyone knew the McCarthys wouldn't join in the annual block party and eventually people stopped inviting them.

But now Maddie saw a woman with an upturned face, thin in the cheeks, with bright eyes as dark as her sons. She was slight of build, enough to make Maddie pause, but her expression was kind, and not at all unwelcoming.

"Oh. Hello. I'm—"

"You're Maddie Conway!" Mrs. McCarthy smiled warmly at her. "I recognized you right away. I see you coming to your father's house through my window every once in a while."

Maddie felt a rush of guilt. "Not as often as I'd like," she admitted.

"Life gets busy. That's how it should be for you young people. I'm always telling my Cole, get out, go! Don't sit around here with me!"

Maddie swallowed hard as she considered her next move. "Is Cole…here by any chance, Mrs. McCarthy?"

"Myrna, please." Cole's mother shook her head. "Cole went next door to help my neighbor with her sink. Leaky faucet. But he'll be back soon if you'd like to wait?"

Maddie nodded as she crossed the threshold into the hallway. She left her boots near the door and handed over the box of cookies. "I made these this morning."

"From your bakery?" Myrna took the box.

"No, um, from my kitchen." Maddie shrugged, but from the way Myrna's eyes lit up, she knew that the implication had been clear. She'd made them especially for Cole.

"Cole tells me that he's been working at your bakery." She smiled. "He said you're quite talented and have excellent taste."

Maddie felt her cheeks flush and she couldn't fight off a smile. "I try."

"Well, come with me to the kitchen. We still have some coffee warming on the burner if you'd like a cup."

It wasn't until Maddie was in the sunlit kitchen at the back of the house that she saw how pale Cole's mother looked. There were dark circles under her eyes and her hands seemed to shake as she reached for a mug.

"I can help," Maddie said eagerly. She slid another glance at Myrna as she backed away, not even putting up a protest.

Unease stirred in Maddie's gut, and memories of a time in her life that she didn't like to remember came to the surface. Cole's mother was not well. And she of all people knew how that felt.

She made two mugs of coffee and sat down at the table with Myrna. Her eyes drifted around the room, searching for something that wouldn't bring up such difficult and worrisome thoughts, and landed on the framed photos on the baker's rack in the corner.

Myrna saw her admiring the photos and commented, "My neighbor says that I have a shrine to my son, but I don't think there's anything wrong with being a proud mother."

"None at all!" Maddie smiled. Idly, she wondered if Myrna knew about all the trouble Cole had caused at school. About the reputation that Cole had even admitted to.

Instead, she said, "I like the one of him holding the fish. Did he catch that?"

"What's that?" Myrna squinted across the room at the photograph that Maddie was referring to, and then seemed to smile at the memory. "His dad used to take him fishing. Cole was especially proud of that catch."

Maddie frowned in surprise, unsure of what to stay. "I'm sorry, I…Cole never mentioned his father," she finally said.

Myrna nodded slowly as she wrapped her hands around her mug, seeming to have more interest in using the coffee to warm herself than to drink it. "His father left when he was only ten. It was a rough age for a boy to be without a father. Cole never got over it, I'm afraid." She sighed. "These things happen, of course, but Cole took it to heart. He and his father were close, you see. His father was a contractor, used to take Cole along on all his jobs. Made him his apprentice of sorts."

Maddie considered this information. The work that Cole had done at the bakery. The way he had denied ever learning anything from his father.

"I'm sorry to hear that," she said softly, and she was. Sorry to hear that Cole was still in such pain that even now, all these years later, he wanted to deny those memo-

ries rather than hold onto them. Sorry that she had mis-
judged him, and that the entire town seemed to do the
same. That all they saw was an angry boy, intent to hurt.
Not a boy who was very much hurting himself.

"Time goes by. Wounds heal," Myrna said, but Maddie
wasn't so sure about that. Even now, more than fourteen
years after her mother had left her life, her heart still felt
heavy when she thought of how much she missed her,
and how much her mother had missed.

"They do," she said. "We learn to move on. But there
are some things we carry with us."

Myrna lightly rested her hand on Maddie's for a moment, before pulling it away. "I remember your mother.
She was very kind."

"She was," Maddie said, feeling her heart tug. "I...I
didn't realize you knew her."

"Oh! Of course! Back when your oldest sister was still
a baby, a group of us ladies used to get together once a
week. We'd take turns, at each other's homes." Myrna's
smile turned a little sad as she reached for her coffee and
took a tentative sip. "When things in my life turned a little
difficult, I found an excuse to leave the club, you see. Life
in this house was...unpredictable. If I couldn't host, I
couldn't impose."

Maddie stared at Myrna, realizing now how different
reality had been from the perception. "My mother would
have welcomed you any day!"

"Oh, I see that now. Now that I'm older and wiser.
But back then...." Myrna shook her head. "Well, it's too
late now. And Cole, well, he's just the same really. I try to

tell him to learn from my mistakes, but maybe it's just in our nature to retreat when times get tough rather than reach out."

Maddie thought of that silent, sullen boy at the bus stop, and the grown man she now knew who went quiet, who had upped and left the pub last weekend without a word or explanation. She tried to think of something to say in response that wouldn't be too prying when there was a scuffling sound at the front door, and Myrna perked up a bit in her chair.

"That will be Cole."

Maddie turned, waiting, as she heard Cole open a creaky door and close it—the closet—and then there he was. She smiled up at him but he looked away, his eyebrows pulling.

"Maddie made us some delicious cookies," Myrna said. She stood to fetch another mug for Cole but he frowned deeply.

"I'll get it. You...sit," he finished. He glanced in Maddie's direction, but away again before he had time to catch her smile.

Sensing that her timing was off, Maddie pushed back her chair. "I was just stopping by on my way to visit my father, so I should probably get along now."

Cole's back was to her, big and strong, and she saw him hesitate for a moment, but he didn't turn around, didn't ask her to stay, or try to change her mind.

He was retreating again. Shutting down.

Myrna got to her feet, and Cole hurried toward her to help. Maddie pretended not to notice that anything was amiss when it clearly was. She wanted to offer to help, to do something, but Cole was a private person, and this was something he had chosen not to share with her.

"It was lovely to see you, Mrs. McCarthy," she said with a little smile when she reached the front door. She almost wasn't sure she should even say anything to Cole, but when she shrugged on her coat and turned around, it didn't exactly matter. He'd gone back to the kitchen.

Myrna reached out and clasped one of Maddie's hands in hers. They shook a little.

"Cole has a kind heart," she emphasized. "And I can see that you do, too. Just like your mother."

Just like her mother.

Maddie held onto those words as she stepped back out into the chilly autumn air, no longer feeling so energized by the snap of leaves under her feet.

She wasn't sure what touched her more. That she was just like her mother, or that Cole was a lot more like her than she'd ever known. Or maybe, tried to know.

*

Maddie was relieved to see her father sitting on the front porch when she arrived, a steaming mug in his hand that was no doubt his third or fourth cup of coffee of the day.

"Well, this is a pleasant surprise," he remarked as she made her way up to the creaking steps.

"I was in the area." She blinked rapidly as she sank down onto the old swing that creaked under her weight from years of use. Her father passed her a blanket from his lap but she motioned it away. "I love the chill in the area. It makes everything seem fresh and…alive."

"You sound just like your mother," Dennis said with a wistful smile. "That woman loved nothing more than the change of seasons. She would declare each to be her favorite."

Maddie thought about that for a moment. "It's true; she always loved the start of summer."

"But then she loved the winter. The more snow, the better." Dennis shook his head. "I hadn't even thought about that until now."

"It's easy to forget," Maddie said quietly. Sometimes, it was easier to forget. But she wanted to hold on, not push the past behind her like Cole seemed to want to do.

She pulled in a breath, thinking of how they'd just left things, wishing she hadn't bothered to stop by at all.

Perhaps sensing her thoughts, her father said, "You coming from the McCarthy house?"

Maddie met his eyes. "I had something to drop off. Cole is helping with the bakery, you know."

"Oh, I know!" Dennis gave a hearty laugh, and Maddie could only roll her eyes skyward. "Don't be too mad at Candy, honey."

"Too mad?" She gave her father a pointed look. "What are all these little projects that Candy has Gus doing here at the moment? Such pressing repairs that couldn't wait until after my bakery was finished?"

Dennis looked at her mildly and took another sip of his coffee. "You and I both know this was never about repairs."

"Right." They agreed on one thing. "It was about Candy wanting to meddle in my love life."

"She just wants to see you happy."

"Who said I'm not happy?" Maddie cried, only right now, leaving Cole on terms like that, she didn't feel happy at all. Yesterday, when he'd almost kissed her, then she'd felt happy. Spent the rest of the festival laughing and chatting with family and friends, but her heart was somewhere else.

And her mind…Her mind should be only on the bakery right now.

"I need to focus on the bakery, Dad. You know how much work it is to run your own business."

Dennis's eyebrows shot up. "Oh, I know, all right. Don't you mind Candy. She's just trying to help."

Maddie grumbled under her breath. She wasn't up for a coffee right now, but she had half a mind to walk in the house and get a mug to warm her up. Instead, she stuffed her hands into the pockets of her coat.

"Speaking of help," Dennis said, "there was a young lady at the festival looking for work. Britt isn't planning to hire anyone new for the off-season, but she might be a good hire for you. She's Franny Benson's granddaughter. Just finished college, doesn't know what she plans to do yet, and she's staying up here for a while until she figures it out. She might not be a long-term fit, but she could work out for now. And you know how Blue Harbor has a way of keeping people here."

Maddie gave a little smile. She knew, all right. "Does she have any baking experience?"

"She's Franny's granddaughter," Dennis said, and that was really all that needed to be said. Franny had always gone head to head with Maddie's mother for every pie baking contest the town ever held.

"I'll call Britt later and ask for the contact information." If this girl was available tomorrow, she'd interview her properly. Already, she was hoping it would work out and she would have one less thing to worry about when it came to her bakery.

Only right now, the only thing that seemed to be troubling her was the thought of Cole, and where they stood.

"Thanks for the help, Dad," she said, standing to give him a peck on the cheek.

"I didn't realize I'd given any," he said, his eyes twinkling. "But I'll gladly give it if you'll take it."

Maddie thought about what he'd said, and she thought about her conversation with Cole yesterday, too. "We're family," she said. "I'm always happy to receive the help."

Even, she considered, when it came from Candy.

11

Maddie hadn't come by the bakery on Monday, not even to check on the progress. Cole didn't read too much into this. A part of him was relieved. The other part...Well, there was no sense dwelling on the other part. Maddie was a sweet girl, always had been, but it stopped there. It always stopped there. With Maddie. With anyone. There was no sense in trying to get close to anyone in this town. And he'd made damn sure that it was impossible, hadn't he?

But the next day, Cole was pulling some tools from his truck when he saw Maddie pulling up on her bike. He knew he shouldn't be mad at her; after all, how was she supposed to know that his mother was sick? It wasn't something he shared. Wasn't something he wanted to admit. Wasn't something he wanted people to know, so he wouldn't have to talk about it.

Hadn't there been enough talk in this town for his family?

But it wasn't fair to come down on Maddie, he knew.

He held up a hand as she came down the gravel path, and when she caught his eye, for a moment he thought she was going to hit the boulder that she was quickly coming up on. But she jerked her handlebar to the left and narrowly missed slamming into the side of his truck. Her cheeks were bright red as she hopped off her seat, and Cole did his best to stifle a laugh.

Unfortunately, it would seem that he hadn't done a good enough job.

Maddie glared at him, her mouth pinched as she swiped her toe across her kickstand.

"Sorry, sorry," he said, trying to hide his grin. "But for a moment there, I thought you were going to wipe out."

"No thanks to you," she said ruefully, but she seemed to be smiling too. "One of the hazards of living in a town this small. Some people have car accidents. I…have bike crashes."

"You mean?" He stared at her, wondering if he was understanding her correctly.

She shrugged. "What can I say? One day I can point out the scars if you'd like." Her cheeks flushed again as their eyes locked, and she glanced away, stuffing her hands into the pockets of her down vest. "I mean, you know, before you finish the job."

"Which should be any day now," Cole said, wanting to deliver good news, but the words fell flat and landed heavily. And for reasons he couldn't explain, he was already starting to dread the day that he finished up here. Sure, he'd have more time to paint the house before the cold front blew in. And he'd have more time to spend with his mother too.

But being here these past two weeks with Maddie had been a welcome distraction. And a surprisingly nice time.

"I was just going to take a break for lunch," Cole explained. There was a pause as Maddie nodded. Cole usual-ly brought his lunch from home, but he hadn't made it to the grocery for supplies in a few days. He knew it would be easy to place an order at the café next door, take it out to his truck, and eat by himself as he usually did, with the radio for company. But he didn't feel like being alone right now. And he suspected that Maddie didn't either. Things had been awkward on Sunday, and he'd seen the way she'd looked at him. It was a look he was all too fa-miliar with growing up. He'd let her down.

But he'd let himself down too.

"Care to join me?" he asked before he thought the better of it.

He pulled in a breath, waiting for her to give him a snappy retort, and rightfully so. He couldn't argue that it was exactly what he deserved.

Instead, she gave him a slow smile, one that made his stomach relax and his heart speed up.

"Sure. What did you have in mind?"

"We could get something from the café?" he offered. It was right next door, after all, and he knew how much Maddie loved supporting her sister's business.

"Only if we take it to go," she warned. "I really can't handle Candy again. I'm still recovering from Saturday."

Cole closed the door to his truck and laughed. "Some-thing tells me that Candy would love nothing more than to see you again."

Maddie considered this as they walked around the building to the café. "She'd love nothing more than to be a part of the family. A permanent part."

"Ah." Cole definitely had that impression, too. He just hadn't considered that maybe Candy was the only one hoping for that outcome. "And I take it that you want something else?"

Maddie gave him a long look, her expression turning wistful. "I guess what I want doesn't really matter, does it? If it isn't possible?"

Cole was about to ask what she meant by that when Candy herself came bursting out of the blue-painted door to the café just before he could reach for the handle. At the sight of them together, her eyes burst open, and a huge smile took over her face.

"My! Look at what we have here!"

"Just grabbing a sandwich," Maddie said mildly. She slanted him an apologetic glance.

Cole didn't mind. He was actually quite enjoying watching the way Maddie squirmed under Candy's overt suggestions. Made up for all the pushing that he had to endure last night from his mother, who seemed determined to stay on the topic of Maddie long after she had left for the day and long after he had stopped answering her dozens of questions.

"A lunch date!" Candy exclaimed.

"No," Maddie ground out. "Just…lunch."

Now her cheeks seemed to positively flame as bright as the red in the sweater that she wore under her vest. Candy, however, seemed completely unaware as she squeezed her hands together and beamed. "Isn't this lovely? You might be able to snag the table near the fireplace if you hurry. In fact, I could always go in and pretend to clean it, to make sure that someone else doesn't snatch it up first? Amelia keeps asking me to come out here and tend to the mums, but really, I've already checked on them a good five times since I punched in this morning! If I didn't know better, I might just think she was getting tired of my singing in the kitchen!"

This time, Cole was grateful that Maddie didn't slide him a look. He wasn't sure he'd be able to compose himself.

"I didn't realize that there was a fireplace at the café," he said to Candy, recalling never having seen such a thing the last time he was here.

Candy gave a knowing smile as she set a hand to her heart and said, as humbly as she could muster, "Actually, that was my idea."

"You had a fireplace installed?" Maddie asked. Her jaw was slack.

As a contractor, Cole knew that this was far from a small project, so he was more than a little curious about how this had taken place. "Oh, is that the project you had Gus doing for you?"

Candy darted her eyes at that, seeming to stumble over her own story as she said, "Oh, no, he's doing some work at the house…The back fence…"

"We don't have a back fence," Maddie cut in.

"Well, we were thinking of getting one. For the dog," Candy added.

"We don't have a dog!" Maddie cried. "Do we?"

"Well, we were thinking of getting one," Candy said. "A fluffy little white one? Oh, I already plan to name it Baby." Her eyes shone.

Maddie blinked a few times and seemed to shake her head, unable to even keep up with the story. "So back to the fireplace."

"Oh." Candy swallowed hard. "Well, it's more of a…space heater? But it looks like a sweet little fireplace, and so I told Amelia that we could make it a special table. You know, really create some *romantic* ambiance, for those chilly days, when you might want to…snuggle?"

Maddie's mouth gaped, and there was a long silence, before she finally said, "Actually, we're grabbing our food to go. Big project. Not much time! I'll let you get to those mums now, Candy!"

Candy winked at Cole as she walked by him and whispered, "I'm still working on that one, but I'm not giving up. Some things are worth the effort." She winked at him again and then disappeared around the side of the building to the window boxes.

"What are you laughing at?" Maddie asked when he met her inside the café a moment later.

"To be honest, I'm not sure if I'm laughing about the dog that doesn't exist or the fence that doesn't exist. Just what does she have Gus working on?"

"I think we both know the answer to that," Maddie told him. She gave him a knowing look. "Probably nothing. Little things here and there, to make sure he was too busy to get the job done for me. Anything to make sure that he wasn't my contractor and you were."

"You mad about that?" he asked.

She gave him a little smile. After a beat, she said, "No."

149

He smiled. It wasn't often he had a compliment. Wasn't often he sought them out.

Or paid them back, he thought.

"Me either," he said with a grin.

*

When they'd collected their sandwiches, cookies, and drinks, which Cole had insisted he pay for, and which of course had prompted the otherwise professional Amelia to flash a look of total excitement on Maddie, they headed down along the lakefront path, both seeming to search for a less public place without saying it aloud.

Maddie didn't have to read into his motives, and she doubted he was either. Cole was a private person. A recluse, even. And she was fairly certain that both Amelia and Candy had their noses pressed against the café windows at the very moment.

She couldn't get out of sight soon enough.

"We could try the docks over near the bay," Cole offered as if reading her thoughts. "I've got a blanket in the back of my truck."

She nodded. She never went over there, but she was familiar with the area, and it wasn't too far. Besides, she liked the walk. The crisp air with a rustle of leaves. She smiled as she held her face up to the sky, feeling the sun against her skin. "Smells like fall."

He looked at her as if he had no idea what she meant. "Smells like fall?"

"You know," she said, squinting at him. Surely, he had to know! "Leaves and a tang in the air, and…and the smell of chimneys, burning their logs."

"I suppose I never thought about any of that before." Cole shrugged, but he looked amused as he pulled a thick blue cotton tarp from the back of his truck.

"I love fall," Maddie said. "I love summer, don't get me wrong, but there's something special about the weather turning, and the tourists leaving, and everyone retreating back inside." She shrugged, a little embarrassed by this admission as they walked down the lakefront path. "Guess you could say I'm a bit of a homebody."

"Is that why you like to bake?"

They had reached the dock and he motioned for them to turn down it. She nodded, following along, happy to see that there was no possible way that Candy could see them now, even with a set of binoculars. They were nestled in an inlet, where the lakeshore had turned, and the trees were dense.

"I always baked with my mother," Maddie said as Cole spread out the blanket and they settled on the dock. She pulled her sandwich from the bag—chicken salad, Amelia's secret recipe that only she was privy to unless Candy was now aware of the addition of cream cheese in the mayonnaise—and peeled back the wax paper from half. "It was sort of our thing, and I kept it going after she…" She still couldn't bring herself to say it, even now, after all these years. "After she was gone."

She felt a lump swell up in her throat and her eyes prickle and she really wished that she had worn sunglasses.

"I'm sorry," Cole said quietly.

The whole town knew, of course, but it was oddly

comforting that he was aware. "It was a long time ago," she said quietly. More than half her life had now been spent without her mother, even though she was still such a part of her.

"Doesn't make it any easier," Cole said, and something seemed to hitch in his tone.

Maddie got the sense that he was about to say something more and then thought the better of it.

"Candy seems determined to be a part of the family, but it's hard to think of another woman in our lives. My mother was irreplaceable," she added.

"She'll always be your mother. I don't get the impression that Candy wants to replace her."

Maddie considered this for a moment as she bit into her sandwich. Candy wanted to be included, but that was different than being a parent. "I'm old enough to not need a mother anyway," she said.

Cole gave her a glance of disapproval. "I find that hard to believe. Everyone needs their parents. Even when they're gone. Especially when they're gone." He drew a breath and looked out over the lake. They fell silent for a long time, as they ate.

"I'm sorry," Maddie said, seeing an opportunity to speak up rather than just let what happened yesterday slip away. "About stopping by your house yesterday."

"I should be the one apologizing," Cole said, giving her a little smile. He set his sandwich down, heaved a sigh. "I'm not used to having visitors. Or…letting anyone in, I suppose."

"To your house?" Maddie asked. Then, because she

saw no holding back now that they were clearing the air, "Or your life?"

"They're one and the same, but I'm a private person. Always have been. When I was younger, I didn't know how to keep everything inside and what came out...Well." He raised his eyebrows, and despite the circumstances, even Maddie had to give a small laugh.

"You were unhappy," she said slowly. "I see that now."

"Not so easy for kids to see," Cole said, setting his jaw. He picked up his food again, took a hearty bite. "Some of the teachers saw through it, though. Some tried to help." He shook his head. "I still feel guilty for what I put my mother through."

"You were hurting. I understand. It's not easy to lose a parent." Maddie held her breath, wondering if she had overstepped, but Cole just stared pensively out at the lake.

"Yeah," he finally said. "Only I didn't lose my father. He left."

"It's still a loss," Maddie said.

"It's not the same." Despite the firmness in his tone, there wasn't any anger. Only sadness.

"Your mom told me about it," she said.

"I figured." His look was wry. "She liked you, you know."

Maddie couldn't help but feel flattered by this. "I liked her. It's clear she adores you. Her eyes practically shone when she said your name."

Cole groaned, but she could tell by the smile in his eyes that he was pleased. "Only child syndrome, I suppose."

"Proud mother syndrome," Maddie replied. She paused, wondering if she should address the real elephant in the room, the fact that once again, something big, and not good, was going on in Cole's life, and just like when he was a child, he was choosing to hold it in, rather than open up and let someone help.

She wanted to help.

Because she of all people knew how it felt.

"Cancer?" She didn't dare look at him. Her heart squeezed tight just thinking of how she'd felt, all those years ago, when the reality that she was going to lose her mother was sharp and raw. It was terrifying and unbearable, and the dread sometimes felt scarier than the thought of a future without her mother in it.

"How'd you guess?" Cole eventually asked.

Maddie looked up, seeing the sadness that now hooded his eyes, and felt her heart pull for him. "Personal experience."

"It's not easy," Cole said, looking out over the water.

"No," Maddie replied firmly. "It's not. But...I'm here, you know. I get it. It's like you said, I was lucky to have the support of all my sisters and cousins and my aunt and uncle. It can't easy for you."

Cole shrugged. "I manage. That's what you do, right?"

Maddie didn't know whether to press the topic, but she felt the need to. For the boy he'd once been. For the man he now was. For the little girl who had tried to reach out to him, but maybe not hard enough.

"There's an entire community here, too, Cole. You know that, right? I mean, Blue Harbor is small. Everyone knows your business, sure, but they also care." Sensing that he didn't buy into any of this, she hesitated a moment before saying, "I care."

She waited for him to protest, to make an excuse, to push away the words or even her. To stand up, to leave.

Instead, he looked at her, really looked at her, for what felt like minutes but was probably only seconds, but all too soon, he was leaning in, and she was leaning in, and then his mouth was on hers, warm and firm, slow and sure, and oh, he was kissing her. And he was a very good kisser.

She pulled back, looking him in the eye, feeling suddenly just as shy and a little out of place as he might have at times. This was new territory for her, even more uncertain than the bakery, but it was just as exciting too.

And it was something she wanted, she realized, as she gave him a slow smile.

"Well, that was a surprise," he said, laughing lowly, taking a big bite of what remained of his sandwich as he inched a little closer to her and turned his gaze to the water.

"There've been a lot of surprises lately," Maddie replied. And all good ones, too.

12

Maddie couldn't believe how quickly the bakery was transforming into a space of her own. Cole had left her a message the following morning that he'd be working with another contractor to install the glass display case that day, and once that was finished, the only thing that would need to be done was to add the light fixtures and hang the sign that he had ordered for her.

The project was nearly finished, and so was their time together. Only after yesterday's kiss, Maddie wasn't so sure that was entirely true.

A little over a month ago, the idea of running her own bakery was a distant dream, and the thought of finding love in this small town seemed almost more impossible. Now, both were within reach. Her life felt full and exciting, and not in a bad and scary way.

Knowing all too well that the old saying "too many cooks in the kitchen" applied when it came to this massive installation, she decided to stay clear of the bakery today, secretly relieved for the opportunity to have some time away from Cole to process everything that had happened yesterday. After their lunch, she'd gone home; it had seemed too awkward to go back to the bakery, working side by side, especially when she was technically his...boss?

No, she wasn't his boss. But she was going to be the boss to someone, and maybe more than one someone. And the sooner she had this part of her business plan sorted out, the sooner she could start to relax. She had interviewed Franny Benson's granddaughter on Monday and quickly discovered that it would be a good fit; Maddie would start training Amy over the weekend. But she'd need at least one more person on a part-time basis, and for backup.

The newspaper office was just ahead, in a small, converted house just past the Town Hall. She caught a glance of Matt walking down the steps as she approached, and slowed her pace.

"How's the bakery?" he asked.

"You should see how it's all coming along!"

"You seem much more relaxed about it all than the last time I saw you," he observed.

She nodded, feeling that his assessment was accurate. She wouldn't say that she was confident, but she was close. And she was at least enjoying the experience, not fretting and losing sleep.

The only sleep she'd lost last night had been on account of that kiss.

She pulled in a breath, forcing her thoughts back to the present.

"Well, I have you to thank for helping set this all in motion."

Matt brushed a hand through the air, but she could tell by his grin that he was pleased. "I was just heading over to steal Amelia away for a coffee break. You want to join me?"

157

Maddie knew how busy Amelia was, and how little time it left for her to spend with Matt. She shook her head. "I have to get over to the newspaper so I can get my help wanted ad in before they go to print. If I have half the success that Amelia has had, I won't be able to run that bakery all on my own."

Matt leaned in, his eyes glimmering with amusement. "Don't you sort of love that we live in a town where people still read the local newspaper every day?"

Maddie laughed. "I do. It's one of the reasons I never left."

"One of the reasons I'm glad I'm back to stay." He shrugged. "Well, I'm off. The main reason to stay is waiting for me as we speak."

Maddie grinned as she watched him walk off in the direction of the café. He loved her sister. Always had. And she was happy for them both.

And maybe, she had reason to be happy for herself now, too.

Maddie pressed on to her destination, admiring the colorful clusters of mums that lined the sidewalks and flanked the door to the white, clapboard house with the cedar-shingle roof. A bell greeted her as she pushed through the paned glass door and entered the offices of the *Harbor Herald*.

Rita Thompson looked up from her computer and smiled. "Maddie Conway! Haven't seen you in a while!"

It was true. Rita had been a good friend of her mother's, once upon a time, and the women used to stick together at all the school events since Rita's daughter was the same age as Britt.

"I hear you're opening a bakery!"

Maddie nodded proudly as she retrieved the printed ad from her tote and spread it on the counter. "That's actually while I'm here. I wanted to post this in the Help Wanted section of the classifieds. I'm not too late to make tomorrow's paper, am I?" She glanced at the clock on the wall.

"That won't be a problem at all," Rita assured her, taking the paper and glancing it over. "I might tighten some of this up for the sake of space, but your contact information will all be there."

"Thanks," Maddie said as her heart began to thump, much as it had when she'd offered Amy Benson a position. Once she officially opened, she'd be responsible, have to pay staff, hold up her end of the promise she'd make them in bringing them on. It was one thing to let herself down, but once someone else was included, she wouldn't be alone in this anymore.

Though, come to think of it, she hadn't felt alone in it since Cole came along.

She smiled.

"Your mother would be so proud of you," Rita said, her smile turning a little sad. "I always said no one could bake like Betsy Conway!"

"I certainly have big shoes to fill," Maddie agreed.

Rita gave her hand a reassuring pat. "I'm sure it will be a huge success. And I want to be the first in line. What day does it open?"

"Next Tuesday. At least, that's the plan." It was all happening so quickly. Maddie felt the old panic rear again and pushed it back into place. "Cole is installing the display case today. Then there will just be a few little finishing touches." She gave a braver smile than she felt. Would everyone else love it as much as she did? Would everyone else like what she baked?

She knew that her mother would have been proud. Of course she would have. But would she agree with Maddie's choices? Was it what she would have done?

"Oh, Cole McCarthy!" Rita smiled, but not in the suggestive way that Candy or Cole's mother had. "My daughter was just mentioning him this morning. Guess he asked her to meet for a drink tonight once he got off the job. Well, now we know what that job is!"

Rita laughed lightly, but Maddie felt her smile slip. Lanie was pretty and single, and a successful real estate agent in town. It was no secret that her good looks helped her with the out-of-town investors who got so swept up in their summer getaway that they decided to buy something seasonal.

"Cole always struck me as being a bit…rough around the edges," Rita confided, lowering her voice. She widened her eyebrows. "But then, people can change, right? They can surprise you."

They certainly can, Maddie thought, blinking back the sting in her eyes.

"And of course, Lanie isn't getting any younger. She's a career woman, and I'm proud of all she's accomplished, but I'd love to see her find someone who makes her happy. It's not exactly easy in a small town like this. But then, I suppose you understand that." She smiled.

"All too well," Maddie said, pinching her lips. She swallowed the lump in her throat. "How much do I owe? For the ad? I was hoping to run it through the weekend."

Rita shook her head. "Your money is no good here, Maddie. You are my dearest friend's daughter, and I know how difficult it is to start a new business. Consider me your first fan."

Now Maddie really felt the tears start to well, and backed away, managing a thick smile. "Thank you, Mrs. Thompson. You're too sweet."

"I'll tell Lanie I saw you!" Rita called after her, as Maddie pushed hard at the door she had just come through.

Maddie managed a nod and stood on the porch as the door closed behind her, taking in big gulps of crisp, autumn air.

Cole was going out for drinks. Tonight. With Lanie.

And she had kissed him. Yesterday. Dared to think that it had meant something. That there was—what? A future? With Cole?

She'd tried to believe that history didn't repeat itself. That each day was fresh. That the future was separate from the past.

That people could change.

She should have known not to get ahead of herself, that things didn't always work out, and that she was in over her head.

That she couldn't trust her own gut.

Or even her own heart.

*

Maddie couldn't bear to go back to the bakery, not now. Not when now every inch of it bore Cole's mark. It felt nearly as much a part of him as it did her. And she'd liked that. Let it happen. Liked the camaraderie.

The encouragement.

Instead, she marched to the flower shop. Even though she hadn't planned on it, when she saw it, she couldn't pass it by. Gabby was filling a watering can when Maddie burst in. She knew she probably looked as wild as she felt, and one glance at her cousin confirmed it.

She was grateful to see that she was alone in the shop.

"Is everything okay?" Gabby set down the watering can, giving Maddie her full attention.

"You know those romance books you love so much?" Maddie demanded.

"Oh, now, don't get in between me and my happy endings," Gabby chided, but her smile dropped when she saw that Maddie was serious.

"Who says that everyone gets a happy ending? Like it's some guarantee?"

"Okay." Gabby held up her hands. "Start at the beginning. What's going on?"

Maddie walked around the counter and dropped onto one of the stools at the worktable where Gabby could arrange her bouquets while manning the storefront. Her eyes welled up as she picked up a particularly lovely rose in the palest shade of yellow. The color immediately made her think of the walls of her bakery. The color that Cole had encouraged her to pick.

Or maybe, the one she had chosen, and that he had agreed with wholeheartedly?

She set the flower down. "I never should have let Candy convince me to hire Cole."

Gabby pursed her lips. "I suspected it had something to do with him. Although, I don't think that Candy left you much choice. And I thought things were working out with Cole? But then, things did seem a little…weird that day at the pub."

"Exactly," Maddie said. She shook her head, wondering why she hadn't seen it before. Cole was anything but predictable. He was moody and quiet.

And sweet. She looked at the rose again, thinking of how he had actually seemed to care that she chose a color for her walls that she would be happy with.

"But you guys seemed so…well, close, I guess, at the Harvest Fest."

"He kissed me," Maddie blurted.

Gabby's eyes widened to giant circles. She didn't speak for what felt like an eternity, and when she did, she couldn't suppress her smile.

"Maddie!" She gave her a fake swat on the arm. "And you didn't tell me? Come on. Every detail. Now."

"It doesn't matter," Maddie said, shaking her head. "I was just talking to Rita Thompson, and she told me that Lanie is having drinks with Cole. Tonight."

Gabby chewed her lip and leaned into the counter. Her gaze drifted to the side, as it did whenever she was hatching a plan, like the times when they were younger and all the cousins would sleepover, and Gabby was always thinking of a way to spice things up, whether it be with more snacks from the pantry or, later, calls to the cuter boys in school, even if she did usually lose her nerve and hang up as soon as someone answered.

"How do you know that they're not just friends?"

Maddie gave her cousin a long, hard look. "Friends? Cole doesn't have friends in town." Only that wasn't true, was it? She was his friend. At least, she had been. Now she wasn't sure what they were.

Boss and employee. God, she should be ashamed of herself!

"Besides," she said, remembering the horrible excitement in Rita's eyes. "Rita seemed pretty titillated by this. Like she was excited for her daughter to be asked out for a night."

"Drinks, not dinner?" Gabby looked at her for confirmation. "They're probably going to the pub." Meaning, the Carriage House Inn.

"Probably," she groaned. Though, secretly, Maddie wished that they were going to Harrisons, with its pool tables and beer and dartboards. Then she would know it was nothing more than friends.

"I'll tell you what we're going to do," Gabby said, setting her hands on her hips. "We're going to go to the pub tonight. Have a drink of our own!"

"Gabby! No!" Maddie stared at her in horror, even as the idea started to take hold. She and Gabby did like to meet up whenever they could, and once the bakery opened, she probably wouldn't have as much time for it, at least, not at first.

She shook the temptation away. Nonsense!

"I already know that he's going on a date with another woman. I don't need to sit back and watch it with my own eyes."

"How are you so sure it's a date?" Gabby asked pertly.

Maddie opened her mouth and then closed it. "What else could it be?" she finally asked.

Gabby shrugged. "Only one way to find out."

*

Cole knew as soon as Lanie Thompson walked into the pub that he had made a mistake. A big one. He should have made things more clear when he'd called and asked her to meet him. Should have maybe gone to her office instead of suggesting common ground—but he hadn't wanted to make his business public, and he knew that if someone saw him sitting in a real estate office, talk would start to fly all over town.

Now, he had every reason to believe talk would still fly. Because from the way that Lanie was dressed in tight jeans and high heels and looking at him like she was memorizing every detail of his face, she had completely misunderstood the point of this meeting.

He should have met her somewhere less…social. Coffee at the Firefly Café would have been ideal, but given the way Candy seemed to follow him around with her eyes every time he crossed his path, he suspected that it would have led to more gossip than just striding into the real estate office and sitting right in front of the window, for all of Main Street to see.

"Hey." Lanie was a little breathless as she shrugged out of her coat and hung it on the back of her chair.

Cole hesitated, not sure if he should stand to greet her or remain sitting. He hadn't dated in years, and when he had, it had been casual, short-lived, and always with someone either passing through town for the summer or residing in a neighboring town.

But this wasn't a date. It was a business meeting. And he'd better make that clear as quickly as possible.

Lanie blinked rapidly as she slid into her seat. Her lipstick was fresh and red, and her sweater was low cut and clearly something she had changed into after leaving the office.

He pulled in a breath. Really, this was half the reason why he needed to get out of this town. He'd gone to great lengths to uphold his privacy and now he had created a bigger mess for himself. He longed to move to a city where no one knew him or his background or cared enough to ask any questions.

He smiled tightly, eager to get to the chase. "What can I get you?" he asked as he made eyes with a waiter across the room.

"White wine," she said with a smile.

Cole turned to the waiter. "White wine and uh…" A beer would really take the edge off what was sure to be an awkward way to start a business relationship, but it would probably only fuel the wrong message he had started to send. "A…water. Just water for me."

Lanie frowned slightly, but composed herself quickly, adjusting herself in the chair, wiggling her torso in a rather suggestive way.

"This is a nice surprise," she said, dragging out the words playfully.

Cole supposed he should be flattered. After all, Lanie was an attractive woman. Successful, too. And she was actually interested in having a drink with him, socially, even if that hadn't been the intention when he'd invited her.

He didn't give that too much thought.

"Thanks for meeting me after hours. I would have met you at the office, but I've been busy on a job site."

The frown reappeared on Lanie's forward, and Cole stifled a wince. He'd messed up, royally.

"I'm looking to get some advice, about listing my mother's house. Not now...but eventually. Soon." God, he hated even thinking about it. He paused, let it sink in, and forced himself to keep going. "I'm just trying to plan ahead, you see, and I'd prefer if we could keep this be-tween the two of us."

Lanie's eyes were wide as she stared at him, but to her credit, she nodded curtly and said, "Absolutely. I'm vaguely familiar with the property, but I'd probably have to walk through it to have a better assessment for list price."

"Eventually, yes," Cole said. Now wasn't the time. His mother didn't know. Couldn't know. It would break her heart to think of him selling that house, nearly as much as it broke his heart to think of leaving it. But it would hurt worse to stay.

He frowned and stared at the table.

"You sure you want to sell?" she asked, picking up on

his exact feelings. "Although, a single guy, you might be wanting something closer into town. Near the action." She waggled her eyebrows.

Despite himself, Cole laughed. "I'll be moving out of town, actually." Probably, out of state.

He wavered slightly at the disappointment in her face, the doubts that he'd started to consider creeping back in. The ones he'd been having for a couple of weeks now, ever since he started the project at the bakery.

Ever since he connected with Maddie.

"Lucky you, honestly," Lanie said. "This town is charming, don't get me wrong, but if it wasn't for my booming business, I'd probably be on the next bus to Chicago."

Cole appreciated her banter. It freed his mind from having to think of other things. Things that shouldn't have any bearing on his long-term plans—ones he had made years back, based on a lifetime of experiences.

This town held nothing for him but bad feelings and a worse reputation, not that he could blame anyone but himself for that. He needed a fresh start. A chance to put all this unease behind him.

But that wasn't all it was. And he knew it. It was difficult enough staying in Blue Harbor after his father left town. It would be downright impossible to stay once his mother was gone too.

"Have you thought about where you'd go?" Lanie asked once the waiter had returned with their drinks.

He considered this for a moment. Leaving town was where his plan stopped. The future was wide open, but instead of feeling full of possibility, it suddenly felt strangely empty.

"Nope," he said, shaking his head. "One step at a time. And I'm not going to be listing the house anytime too soon." At least, he didn't hope so. "I just…like to be prepared."

"Responsible," she said. "I wish all my sellers had the same approach. It takes time to get a house ready to sell for top dollar."

"Responsible is a word that few people in town would connect to me." He raised an eyebrow, and she gave a knowing smile in return.

"People grow up," she said, giving him a suggestive look that was his cue to leave.

He leaned back, nodded slowly. He had grown up, he supposed, turned into the kind of son that would make his mother proud. But he wasn't so sure that selling her house would make her happy. It was the first selfish thing he had done in a long time.

It needed to be done, he reminded himself firmly.

Lanie gave a little defeated sigh and raised her glass. "I never shake hands until a deal is closed, but here's a toast. To a…professional relationship."

Cole grin, relieved. "I'll drink to that," he said, now regretting that he'd only ordered a glass of water.

He glanced over to search for the waiter, for something stronger, but his eyes caught something across the bar.

It was Gabby. She was staring at him with the same accusing look that he'd come to know all too well growing up in this town.

And beside her, Maddie.

And just before he could hold up a hand and wave, a crowd of guys he recognized from high school pushed up to the bar, and a moment later, when they cleared, the seats where Maddie and her cousin had sat were empty.

And Maddie was gone.

13

The alarm went off at the same time as usual the next morning, but Maddie was already awake. More like, she'd never fallen asleep.

She brewed a pot of coffee and hugged her robe tighter as she looked out the window onto the sunny, autumn morning. October was her favorite month, technically. The leaves on the maple tree in the backyard wouldn't last much longer, she knew, and so she decided to take her mug out to the small patio table to enjoy the view.

Her robe was warm enough that she didn't need a coat, but she swapped her slippers for her Sherpa-lined boots and ventured out the back door. She was surprised to see that Amelia had the same idea as her.

"Hey!" she said. "You aren't at the café?" Maddie checked her watch to be sure she wasn't the one mixed up—she wouldn't be surprised anymore. Her head was all over the place these days. It was well after six. Amelia was always at the café by now.

And Maddie was happy that she had already made the cinnamon rolls for today when she'd returned from the pub last night, too wound up to sleep.

"Be sure to grab the cinnamon rolls on your way in."

"I'll leave right before we open," Amelia said. "Candy

said she'd get in early today so I could catch up on some stuff around the house this morning. I've run out of time for laundry and errands now that I'm back together with Matt."

Back together was a stretch. They'd been apart for a dozen years. While factual, Maddie knew that it was Amelia's humble way of not stating the obvious.

"You mean, now that you have a boyfriend." Despite the sad state of her own love life, Maddie couldn't help but grin. She loved teasing Amelia. Sure enough, her sister's cheeks turned pink.

"I can see that you're pleased about that." Amelia's smile was rueful. "And now that I have a boyfriend, you can finally get off my back. Actually, maybe I can turn the tables now. Candy seems to think that there might be something going on between you and Cole." She waggled her eyebrows.

"Pfft. Please." But Maddie struggled to make eye contact, and she steeled away from the tears that threatened by taking a slow sip of her coffee. It had come out just right today, the perfect ratio of cream to brown sugar, her favorite combination, but it did little to lift her spirits. "Cole is my contractor, and not by choice, either. And I have no time for a relationship or romance. I'm starting my own business. You know better than anyone just how much time that takes."

Amelia nodded thoughtfully. "I do. And I also know now that it doesn't have to be that way. I poured all my energy and time into Firefly for too many years. Don't get me wrong, I'm proud of that place, and I want it to succeed. But there's such a thing in life as balance, and for a long time, I think I used my career as a crutch."

"How so?" Maddie stared at her sister. It was the first time she'd heard Amelia admit to having any doubts about how she'd run her very successful café.

"It's easy to throw yourself into a business. To believe that every decision you make will lead to success or failure. To feel guilty if you don't get everything right or devote all your time to it." She shrugged. "Some nights are bad. Some months are bad. If I had sat back and recognized that sooner, it would have been a lot more difficult for me to hide behind my café instead of putting myself out there." She grinned. "But then, I suppose I wouldn't be back together with Matt. Anyway, things have a way of working out in the end. *If* you are open to it."

Maddie opened her mouth and then closed it again, nodding as she digested this information. She may not have openly asked for help when it came to her new venture, but that didn't mean she would turn her back on advice that was offered. She was open-minded, she'd learned. Not just with the business, but with people. Most folks in town wouldn't give Cole a second glance, much less a second chance. But she'd seen someone who was genuine and caring, and a far departure from what appeared on the surface.

She thought back to last night, and what Gabby had insisted before they'd gone to the pub, and then left shortly afterward.

Maybe things weren't always as they appeared.

Maybe, when she saw Cole today, she'd learn that there was an entirely plausible (and platonic) reason for Cole to be having drinks with an attractive, available woman.

Or maybe that was wishful thinking again.

*

Despite the anger and confusion that Maddie had felt after last night, she couldn't help but grin ear-to-ear when she arrived at the bakery later that morning, to see her beautiful, gleaming display case installed, and above it, a row of vintage-style pendant lights that she'd chosen to match the sconces that would go on the walls.

The lights were lit, giving a warm glow to the room. Her eyes drifted up to the large space along the back wall, above the counter, where her menu would be hung, her heart thumping at the thought of the carefully chosen selections on display for all to see.

"What do you think?"

Maddie turned to see Cole standing in the doorway, giving her an easy grin. For a moment it was as if nothing had passed between them last night, as if she hadn't seen him, caught him, red-handed, having a drink with another woman just a day after kissing her. His expression showed no trace of guilt. But there was a question in his eyes. Hesitancy she hadn't seen from him before when usually he was so in control of his every emotion.

He'd made sure of that.

She hesitated, knowing how easy it would be to pretend that last night hadn't happened. To go back to the day before instead, when he'd kissed her. Opened up to her. When it felt like they had bonded over more than paint colors and closets and shelving.

When it felt like whatever was forming between them would last longer than the last day of construction on the bakery.

Something in the rigid way he was standing told her that the door had shut. He'd closed off again, just like when he was a kid.

"It's beautiful," she said truthfully.

He nodded but didn't come much farther into the room. "Glad you approve, boss."

He grinned at her, but something in his eyes fell flat. He was trying to keep things friendly, she saw, but his heart wasn't in it.

Maybe, it never was.

"I'm not your—" She sighed. Wondered if she should just go into the kitchen and let him finish what was on the schedule for the day. The sconces. Hanging the sign. Polishing the wooden floorboards. And then…Then it would be over. He'd go and she'd be left with this bakery.

It was all she'd ever wanted once. Now, it didn't feel like enough. It felt like something was missing. Something that she hadn't even known that she wanted.

"I saw you last night," she started again. She tried to keep her tone light and conversational rather than accusatory. After all, he had made her no promises. He was free to have drinks with whomever he pleased. They'd only shared a kiss.

But it felt like so much more than that. And the hurt that crept into her voice revealed her true feelings.

He nodded again, gave her a flash of a guilty grin that threw her. So he wasn't going to deny it? Didn't feel ashamed?

Unless maybe…

"It wasn't a date if that's what you're wondering."

"Oh." She blinked. Felt the breath escape her in a rush of relief that bordered on foolishness. So Gabby had been right. And yet again, Maddie had overanalyzed something. Doubted her own instincts. Lost trust in not only Cole but in herself.

"I would have told you, and I tried to call you over, but you and Gabby seemed to leave before I had a chance." He gave her a long, knowing look.

Maddie felt her shoulders slump as she walked closer to where he stood. "Gabby had to get going," she started, knowing it was a lame excuse and that Gabby was never one to call it a night too soon. Maddie had Cora for that. "And I…Well, you and I had never really talked about what happened between us."

"What happened between us." Cole's eyes locked with hers, his gaze steady, and Maddie could feel the pull, making her chest tighten, making her want to step closer, to feel his arms around her again, pulling her close against the heat of his body.

"That was—"

"A mistake," he said before she had a chance to speak.

Nice. She had been about to say nice.

Now, she was almost relieved he'd cut her off before she'd had a chance to say what she'd intended—and meant. It had been nice to her. Very nice.

And to him, it had been a mistake. Wow.

Sensing the hurt in her face, Cole dragged a hand through his hair, emitting a low groan. "I like you, Maddie. I like you a lot, and…I don't really like a lot of people around here."

"Maybe that's because you never gave them a chance," she said, hearing the hurt creep into her voice. She stared at him, angry, and angry at herself for daring to believe that he was someone different than he was.

Cole looked at the floor, shoved his hands into the pockets of his jeans. "Fair enough. But I've lived in this town all my life, and I made the decision a while back that I was going to leave, first chance I had."

Maddie blinked at him. "So you were meeting with Lanie because she's a real estate agent? What about your mother?"

Hurt flashed in his eyes. "Don't you get it, Maddie? You, of all people? She's the reason I've stayed, all this time. She's the reason I'm still here."

And the reason he would leave.

Maddie pulled in a breath and released it slowly. She could feel her own heartache, mirrored in his face. The horrible sense of impending loss, the fear of what would happen next, the miserable thought of being left behind, without any choice in the matter.

Only Cole did have a choice.

"Sometimes the memories keep people alive," she told him softly. She opened her arms wide, to the room, to this bakery, that she had created only because she had refused to bury every memory of her mother along with her body. "This is all here because I didn't want to put the past behind me. Same goes for Amelia. And Cora. And even Britt."

Only Britt had done a runner. Fled first chance she had. Said she couldn't bear to be in a place where her mother no longer was.

But she'd come back, eventually. And she was happy she had. They all were.

"You have a community here," Maddie told him. "People who know your mother."

Cole shook his head firmly. His jaw was tense. "No, *you* have a community. *You* have a family. I only ever had my mother. And people might know her, but they also know me. And they don't like me much."

"I like you," she said, giving him a little smile. "And Bella over at the bookstore. And Candy." She'd been about to mention Matt and Gabby, but she could tell that he wasn't open to hearing any of it.

That maybe, he wasn't very open to anything. Or anyone.

For a moment she thought she saw a hint of a smile pass over his face, but it was gone all too soon.

"I'm sorry, Maddie. I shouldn't have gotten involved with you. I shouldn't have led you on. Not when I've already made up my mind."

"So that's it then, is it? You won't even consider the possibility of sticking around, seeing if something good can happen in this town?"

"Staying in town wouldn't change anything," he replied.

"What's that supposed to mean?"

He tossed up his hands, exasperated. "Relationships don't last, Maddie. Either they end, or someone dies. Either way, they are over."

"So you'd rather be alone?" She stared at him. "You said you always wished you had more family."

"I wished for a lot of things. For my father to stick around. For my father to come back. For my mother to…" He shook his head. His jaw pulsed.

Maddie took a step toward him, but he backed up. She stopped, realizing that he wasn't going to be swayed. That his mind was made up. That he was determined to be the lonely, angry boy he'd always been, not the man she believed him to be.

"I'll go and let you finish up," she said.

She turned, hating that this space had now become tainted with bad memories and fresh hurt when it was supposed to be her happy place. The best parts of her past. The brightness of her future.

"Maddie." His voice was low but insistent, and she turned slowly, daring to hope for one second that he had changed his mind.

Changed his heart.

But the sadness in his eyes told her more than his words.

"Thank you, Maddie, for everything," he said.

It was the closest she would get to a goodbye.

14

Maddie slept in the next morning, the thrill of going into the bakery had been replaced with the dread of seeing Cole again, and knowing that his mind was made up. That he'd let the past define him. That nothing she could say would change that.

Amelia had already popped in and grabbed the cinnamon rolls from the fridge; Maddie hadn't even stirred, but Amelia had no doubt let herself in the back door and been quick and quiet.

She made coffee in the kitchen, looking out her window as it percolated, to the big maple tree in the backyard that boasted crimson leaves, mixed with orange. She loved that tree. Always said it was one of the reasons she would never move from this apartment, even though she knew that, eventually, she would. Amelia and Matt were getting closer by the day, and it was inevitable that they'd get married, move in together, that they might need more space, want to expand into this garden unit.

Or maybe they would be the ones to move out, and Maddie would be the one to stay, take over the larger owner's unit above. Matt was renovating his old childhood home—surely he'd want to keep it.

Either way, change was inevitable. Life kept moving

along, even when you didn't want it to. The changing of the leaves on the great, big tree was proof of that.

When she'd finished her coffee and finalized her menu for the opening week, she decided that she couldn't put things off anymore. The furniture was being delivered today—the last items on her once daunting checklist—and she had to sign for it.

She changed into a warm sweater and jeans. Pulled her hair into a ponytail. The sky looked a little threatening, so she grabbed an umbrella, but still she rode her bike to the bakery, her eyes tearing against the harsh wind blowing off the lake, or maybe the tears were from something else. Disappointment. Heartache.

Outside the bakery, there was no sign of Cole's truck, and Maddie didn't know whether to be relieved or let down. She checked her watch, noting that it was later than she'd expected. Perhaps he'd gone to lunch already. Perhaps he'd be back soon.

But when she walked into the bakery and flicked on the lights, she knew at once that Cole wasn't coming back at all.

His ladder was no longer propped in the corner, carefully angled against the wall. His toolbox was no longer resting beside it. The job was complete and any evidence that Cole had ever been a part of this endeavor had been swept up and washed away, wiped clean.

It was the fresh start she had longed for, only it no longer felt like the beginning of something. It felt like the end of something.

The sconces were lit, the floorboards were polished.

The great big chalkboard hung over the counter, waiting for her to climb up on a stepstool and add the weekly and daily specials. The glass countertop was gleaming, the polished wood surface waiting to be filled with her daily sweets. There would be pies and brownies and cookies and cakes, and seasonal specials, too. There would be warmth and spices and smells so powerful that no one would be able to resist and everyone would struggle to decide and promise to come back again. She'd have regulars. They'd have their regular tables. She'd learn to know everyone's favorites, just like Amelia did next door. She'd know what sold best and what wasn't worth making the following week.

She'd know what to do. She hadn't believed it, until now, standing in her beautiful bakery. Her vision was complete.

She'd done it, she thought, for one, heart-pounding moment. She'd actually done it!

But that wasn't exactly true, she knew. They'd done it. She and Cole. She couldn't have done it without him.

With a heavy heart, she began unpacking the boxes of cake stands and mismatched teacups and saucers hand-painted with flowers and birds and butterflies. The shelf that lined the back wall of the counter was soon homey and colorful, and Maddie wished that Cole was here to see it. That she could share this moment with someone. That she could share it with him.

Instead, she pressed on. Pulled her menu list from her file and dragged the stepstool from the closet, careful not to scratch any of her shining hardwood planks as she set it up. She climbed to the top step, her chalk marker in hand, almost afraid to mar the surface, even though she knew that was silly. At the café, she always added the specials. Amelia always told her she had lovely handwriting.

With one breath for courage and another glance at the general design she had sketched out on the paper, she got to work, drawing swirls and a pie, a cupcake in another corner, and the simple menu, one that she would grow over time.

She was just stepping off the ladder to admire her work, when Maddie turned at the sound of tires crunching over gravel, her heart speeding up.

"Cole," she breathed. Maybe he had come back. Maybe the work wasn't finished. Maybe he realized that she still hadn't given him his final payment.

Maybe he was coming back to apologize. To say he had changed his mind.

Only it wasn't Cole at all. With a sinking heart, Maddie watched the furniture delivery truck pull to a stop and two men hop out of the front cab. She'd been eager for this furniture since she'd placed the order, knowing that it would be the final finishing of her vision. That once it was set up, the bakery would be complete.

Only right now, everything felt wrong, and empty, even though it was all finished, and it was really, all so right. It had come together. She didn't know how, but it had.

Except that she did know why.
Because of Cole.

*

Maddie stood in a sea of furniture, set in the corner, nearest the door, the tables pushed together, the chairs stacked and scattered. Her pristine new bakery suddenly felt like a complete mess again, in every possible way.

"Yoohoo!"

Maddie turned to see Candy pushing through the tarp that still hung over the doorway to the café until she was officially opened. She froze for a moment, realizing that when she and Amelia had first come up with the idea to join the two establishments, Candy had not been a member of Amelia's staff.

And even then, Maddie had assumed it was a temporary arrangement.

But Candy was right at home at the café, as she was at their father's house, and now Maddie bit back the creeping fear that she would soon be as permanent a fixture at the bakery as the sign over the front door.

Candy's eyes swept over the place dramatically and she held her hands to her mouth, shielding her smile.

Despite the source, Maddie felt herself swell with pride.

"You like it?" She'd considered inviting her family all over together, for a true unveiling this weekend after the market, but seeing as Amelia and Candy were next door most days, that was probably never going to be a realistic option.

Really, Maddie realized that she should be surprised Candy had managed to restrain herself from barging in sooner.

"Like it?" Candy's eyes were round. "This is gorgeous, Maddie! Absolutely stunning! I *love* the wall color."

"That was Cole's doing," Maddie said, hating the hurt that crept into her tone at the mere mention of his name. "Well, he provided the options."

"But you chose the color?" Candy grinned. "You have excellent taste. But then, I'm not surprised. Still, it's even prettier than I pictured."

Maddie felt her stance soften. The compliment was genuine, straight from Candy's heart, and she was starting to see what her father and even Amelia saw in the woman. Candy was happy for her.

Just like her mother would have been.

"Where is Cole today?" Candy asked as casually as she could muster. But the inquisitive look to her gaze was telling.

Maddie sighed. She'd have to shut down Candy's hopes, along with her own.

"He's not here at the moment. I...I think he's finished with the job."

"You think?" Candy stared at her, confused. "Did you give him his final check?"

"Not yet." She didn't know how to handle that part. They hadn't discussed it. And Cole was professional and a gentleman enough not to stand around waiting for it. He either knew she was good for it, or he knew where to find her.

Either way, it meant that he trusted her. She didn't know whether to find comfort or sadness in this fact. There weren't many people in town he trusted, she knew.

"Well, then I'm sure he'll be back," Candy insisted.

Maddie pushed one of the chairs toward the corner of

the room. "Or I can drop the check off at his house this weekend. Put it in his mailbox."

"Well, I live right there," Candy said, and then, catching herself, she said, "I mean, that I'm always there. With your father. I can drop off the check today. I'm happy to help."

Maddie had visions of Candy rapping on Cole's front door, barging in, settling onto the sofa for a nice long chat.

She shook her head. "Thanks, Candy, but I think you've helped enough."

She knew from the hurt in Candy's eyes that she had crossed a line.

She dropped her eyes, sighing. "I'm sorry, Candy. It's just that...I know you sent Cole here for reasons other than helping me set up the bakery."

Candy attempted to feign innocence for a moment, but quickly realized she wouldn't get away with it. "Can you blame me, honey? I see this cute, smart, creative, young woman, and I think...here's a nice, good-looking, single guy. Why not try?"

"But I never said I was looking for love," Maddie pointed out.

Candy dismissed that with a wave of her hand. "Please! Who isn't looking for love?"

"Cole, for starters," Maddie said. She dropped onto one of the chairs, pleased to find that it was quite comfortable. There wasn't any satisfaction in winning this argument with Candy. Cole wasn't interested in love. And he wasn't interested in her.

"Well, now, I saw the two of you together!" Candy said, frowning in concern. She quickly pulled up another chair, close to Maddie. "You seemed to be really hitting it off."

"We were," Maddie admitted. "But…he's closed off. Doesn't want to let anyone in. Never did. Never will."

"People say that," Candy said, dismissing the notion with a wave of her hand. "People even *think* that. But when the right person comes along, everything changes. Look at your father and me!"

Maddie considered this. It was true that her father had seemed closed off to the idea of love after losing his wife. He'd been alone for over a decade and might have been that way forever if he hadn't fallen off that ladder last spring and needed a caretaker.

But there was one telling difference between her situation and theirs. "I don't think I'm the right person for Cole."

"You really believe that?" Candy asked.

Maddie sighed. "Truth be told, I don't think I do believe it. But it doesn't matter what I say. Cole's closed off his heart to this town. He's not willing to give anything about it a chance. Or anyone." She glanced at Candy. "He's planning to leave town first chance he has. Doesn't want to get involved."

"Ah." Candy gave a knowing smile. "Meaning he doesn't want anyone coming along and changing his mind."

Maddie wasn't sure that she liked where this was headed. It was common knowledge that Candy didn't take no for an answer lightly.

"I think his mind is made up," Maddie said firmly. "He's had this planned for a long time now."

"And then you come along and make him start thinking that leaving this town won't be as easy as he thought it would be." Candy's eyes gleamed as she nodded her head.

Uh-oh. This had all the hallmarks of a plan being hatched. Maddie knew that look. All too well. Come to think of it, it was the very same look that Candy had at their last family dinner.

"No, Candy." Maddie shook her head. "No more plans. No more schemes. The man has made up his mind, and I respect that. His mother is very sick. This town has nothing but bad memories for him. I should know how that feels."

Candy's expression softened, but something told Maddie that her stance hadn't.

"Sometimes you have to ask yourself if you're willing to be stuck in the past forever, or if you want to move forward. It sounds to me like Cole has some soul searching to do, and he might not have had to think about any of this until very recently."

Maddie knew this was probably true. That he wouldn't have kissed her if he didn't care.

"Now, you may find this hard to believe, but I'm not one to sit back and let things just…happen. Makes me crazy, really, when there's something I could be doing instead!"

Oh no. Maddie opened her mouth to protest, but Candy just patted her knee. "But in this case, my girl, I think the best thing you can do is nothing."

Maddie balked at her. "Really?"

"You just focus on your lovely bakery, here. You worked hard to make this happen and you deserve to enjoy it."

Maddie gave a weak smile. "Thanks, Candy, I needed to hear that." After all, the entire point of even opening this bakery was to think about her future and to honor her mother. She didn't want to feel like it was tainted by her time with Cole.

She'd rather it be a testament to the fact that good things could always come about from the worst things you'd lived through.

"But there is one thing I can do," Candy said with a gleam in her eye.

Maddie felt her trepidation build again. Warily, she asked, "What's that?"

"Celebrate your opening! What's better than a Sunday family dinner?" She blinked rapidly. "I mean....Sunday dinner?"

Maddie reached over and squeezed Candy's hand. "A Sunday *family* dinner sounds like exactly what I need right now."

*

Cole found his mother sitting at the kitchen table when he came downstairs the next morning, later than usual, and only because he had been up the night before, tinkering in the garage, mostly moving old boxes around and organizing his tools. It was always his hideaway place. The place he'd first come with his father, back when he would watch him work, when it was the one place where his father seemed at ease, and almost happy, even if it was just showing him how to sand down a rough edge on a board. Later, it was the place he came to think about his father. Eventually, it became the one place he could come that was all his own.

He knew people in town talked, wondered why a man his age still lived at home. That was none of their business, and he'd intended to keep it that way. Until Maddie came along.

He pushed her immediately out of his thoughts. The coffee was already brewing and his mother seemed to have more energy than usual. It was one of her good days. A day when he should breathe a sigh of relief, knowing that for a few hours, he might not have to worry—too much.

Instead, he noted the frown on her forehead and uneasily reached for a mug.

"I was starting to wonder if I should wake you," his mother said. A little smile appeared on her lips. "Remember how I used to have to flick the lights to get you out of bed?"

"When I was, like, ten," he replied, but he, too, smiled.

"Never did like going to school," she said with a sigh.

He lifted his eyebrows, turning from her to lift the coffee pot. "No, I suppose I didn't." It wasn't the work that bothered him. It was everything else. The reminder that he was different. That he didn't fit in. And that he wanted to. He just wanted to be ordinary, like everyone else. A kid with a dad who actually loved him.

That he wasn't different. Or alone. Except that some-where along the way, he'd made sure to be alone. Told himself it was better if he chose it, rather than accepted it.

"But then, I never minded having you here," she said, no doubt referring to all the times she'd quietly accepted his excuse of having a headache or stomachache to get out of some class party or school event—field trips or other bonding experiences that most other kids looked forward to every year—and called in his absence.

"Good, because I'm all yours today," Cole said. He filled his mug to the rim, knowing he'd need the caffeine. "I'll run into town for groceries, and then I thought I'd get a start on that painting I promised you."

"You don't have to go into the bakery today?" his mother asked.

"Job's done," Cole said tightly.

There was no denying the shadow of disappointment that fell over his mother's face when he joined her at the table. "Oh. Did it already open?" she asked, glancing at him.

He didn't meet her eye as he drank his coffee. "Tues-day is the opening day, I believe." Maddie had explained that like her sister's café next door, the establishment would be closed on Mondays.

He couldn't help but feel nervous for Maddie, know-ing it would be a big day for her, one that he might have liked to support, had things turned out differently.

He shook off that thought. No sense in going down that path again. Maddie was a sweet person. One of the sweetest he'd met, other than his mother. There was no sense in dragging her down with him. She had a bright future ahead of her. And he…

He didn't know what he had anymore. Maybe, he never did.

"Well, better get to it while the weather holds," he said, sliding back his chair. Through the window, he could see clouds forming in the grey, autumn sky.

"Why are you so insistent on painting this house?" his mother asked. "It looks fine just as it is."

Cole rinsed his mug and set it on the rack to dry.

"The paint is chipping, Mom," he said. It looked tired. It looked mildly neglected. It looked like the house of a family who had other things going on. Bad things.

It spoke the truth. And he…he was trying to cover it up. Deny it. Push it away. Like always. Even when he was a kid, he was forever trying to hide the obvious. When that failed, put up the front. Once he got big enough, he started tending to the house. If there was nothing worth talking about, then maybe people would leave him alone. And maybe, eventually, he'd forget.

"I thought it would make you smile," he said, feeling the tightness in his throat. "I'm just freshening things up."

"And here I thought you were fixing it up to sell," she said, raising an eyebrow.

His hand stilled on the doorknob. He took a moment, considering his words. The last thing he wanted to do was to hurt her. To let her down. His father had done enough of that for the both of them. "Mom. You know that I have nothing for me in this town but you."

She gave a little shrug, but her eyes were sad. "I think you should sell," she surprised him by saying. "You've given up a lot of time taking care of me, Cole."

"You're my mother!" he ground out, but she just held up a hand, silencing him.

"And you're my son." She gave him a stern look. One he hadn't seen since his grade school days when she returned from yet another meeting at the school to discuss his poor performance, the need to maybe repeat a year. He'd hated the defeated and weary look in her eyes back then as much as he did now. And yet again, he vowed he would do better, for her, and this time, he was old enough to keep that promise.

"You're my only child. And I do think you should sell."

His eyebrows shot up. "Really? You're okay with that?"

"You've stayed here long enough, Cole. Get something that is yours. Something that makes you think of the future, and not the past."

"We had some good times in this house," he said, thinking of the few years they had when she was in remission. When hope sprung. When he thought he'd been given a second chance at being a good son. At...everything.

"I brought you home to this house." His mother's eyes watered. "You were the prettiest baby anyone had ever seen. You had such long eyelashes that everyone thought you were a girl."

Cole barked out a laugh. "That's a stretch."

193

"It is now," his mother said, chuckling. She shook her head, marveling at him. "You're a fine man, Cole. The best man I've ever known."

There was a heavy silence, and Cole knew that they were both thinking about another man in their family. A man they never discussed, because the hurt was still too raw.

"Your father and I had some good years…"

Cole didn't want to hear this. "Mom—"

She held up a hand. "Cole, we had some good years. And you did, too. I know that doesn't make up for him leaving us like he did, but…those years were real. They counted. And they happened right here in this house."

Cole thought of the little moments, the memories he'd tried to push away, like the time his father had helped him build a birdhouse, and hung it from the tree out front.

When he'd left, and when it was clear that he wasn't coming back, Cole had climbed that tree all on his own and hacked down the birdhouse, tossing it in the trash. He knew his mother had watched from the window, but she never said a word about it.

Eventually, they never spoke of the topic at all. Until now.

"You were always different, though, Cole," his mother continued. "Your father…he was restless. He never could have stood by my side like you have all these years."

"I'm your son."

"And a good man."

Cole shook his head. He knew where this was going. His mother was thinking of Maddie. He was thinking of

Maddie. Of the hurt in her eyes. The hurt he caused so easily, just like when they were kids. How quickly he could pull the light from her smile.

She was a good person. She had a kind heart. And he... "I'm not husband material."

"Oh, now, don't sell yourself short, Cole." She gave him a pointed look. "You're your own person. Your life is what you choose to make of it."

What he chose to make of it. He hadn't even dared to consider his life, or what he wanted. He'd been too busy getting by, and thinking about getting out. But beyond that escape was a blank canvas.

Only now it was starting to feel more like a vast nothingness.

"Your father ran away, Cole. You don't have to."

He chewed his lip, unable to agree. His head was pounding, and he needed more coffee, but he wanted to get out. To the garage. To the lake. Out of this house.

Away from the truth. Because that's what his mother was telling him, wasn't it? The cold hard truth. And he'd never been good at hearing it or taking it. Even now, when what she was telling him was what he already knew. And yet he still fought it.

Maddie had opened his eyes. And his heart. Showed him that there was more to this town than bad memories. That there could maybe be a future.

He looked at his mother, sitting pale in her chair. He checked himself. Felt that tightening of his resolve. The protective wall came back up. Sure, there could maybe be a future. But there were no guarantees. And luck hadn't ever been on his side.

"I should get started before it rains," he said, reaching for the handle to the back door.

"Go ahead and paint the house," she said. "But if you really want to cheer me up, you'll bring me to the opening of the bakery. I haven't been able to stop thinking about those cookies that Maddie Conway dropped off, and I'm hoping she has more."

"Mom." Cole gave her a long look. They both knew that Maddie's cookies had nothing to do with her insistence on him taking her to the bakery on Tuesday. "Maddie is a very nice woman—"

Before he could finish, she said, "Leave it there, Cole. Some things are what they are, and it's better to accept them than fight them."

He pulled in a breath. She had him there.

"And Maddie is a very, very lovely girl," his mother emphasized.

He gave her a little smile before he walked into the backyard. Yes, Maddie was everything his mother had described. And more.

And some things were what they were. No argument there.

15

Maddie didn't know why she should be so worried about opening the door to the bakery. It wasn't opening day—yet—and her family loved her, and supported her. They wanted her endeavor to be a success more than anyone else in the town. They were her biggest cheerleaders and always had been.

And they were therefore the ones that she wanted to impress the most.

The plan was for everyone to meet at the bakery and then go back to the house on Water Street, where Candy had promised a proper fall meal around the dining room table. Amelia would be sharing her lasagna recipe and Candy would be extending her baking skills to tackling the garlic rolls.

"It can't be cheese biscuits every day," Candy had announced, and Maddie could only stare in surprise, wishing her sisters had been there to share in this proclamation, because she'd come to love sharing everything with her sisters, from their clothes to their businesses to their wisdom.

But it was okay to have something all of her own, too. For once.

With one more breath, she unlocked the door and

opened it, to the smiling faces of her father and sisters, her cousins Gabby and Jenna, and Candy, and her aunt and uncle in the back.

"I've already had the honors," Candy told everyone, "so you all go in first."

Amelia caught Maddie's eye, and Cora suppressed a smile. There was no doubt in any of their minds that had Candy not already been inside the bakery, she would have been leading the pack today.

Or maybe not, Maddie thought, thinking back to her conversation with Candy the other day. Candy wanted to be a part of this family because she didn't feel like part of it. But those days were over. A lot of things were over. And this bakery was living proof that the future was just beginning.

"Oh, Maddie," Amelia breathed. She shook her head in wonder, and Maddie could almost swear she saw tears building in her eyes.

"This is beautiful," Cora agreed, giving Maddie's shoulder a little squeeze.

"I haven't shown you everything yet," Maddie said a little breathlessly after the official tour was over, and they'd all oohed and awed over the kitchen and storage space, and the lights and the furniture.

Amelia had even taken the liberty of removing the tarp between their two establishments.

"Together again," she announced, to everyone's applause. "I wouldn't have it any other way."

Maddie opened the cabinet in the kitchen, showing them the dishes she had carefully selected for the bakery.

"They're just like Mom's!" Cora marveled.

"Now I really feel like a part of her is here," Maddie said, swallowing back the lump that had formed in her throat.

"I can think of something else that will make her here," Britt said. She reached up and pulled the apron from the top shelf, where it was stowed away, still in tissue paper. "It's time for you to officially wear this."

Maddie glanced at all of her other family members, searching for approval, but knowing, deep down in her heart, just like she had always known, that she had it. And she always would.

With a big breath, she slipped the loop over her neck and tied it at her waist.

She was doing this. And it was way too late to turn back now.

Not that she'd even dream of it.

*

By Tuesday morning, the house was painted, the lawn was raked, the coffee was brewing, and Cole was left wondering if his mother would remember that today was Maddie's opening day.

Because it was all that he could think about. He imagined her turning the sign on the door. Standing behind the display case. The tarp now gone. The lights lit. The kitchen alive and busy.

He hoped it was everything she wanted it to be. He hoped that it would be a success and that maybe, he'd helped play a little part in that.

His mother came down the stairs, looking a little rosier in the cheeks, but she said nothing as she eased into her favorite chair near the window and Cole handed her a warm mug. He waited for a beat, to see if she would say anything, and then went about making some toast. He'd gone shopping as promised, in town. He'd seen Lanie who smiled, luckily nothing awkward there. And Bella, who mentioned that she had some new paperbacks his mother might like. He saw Matt, who told him how Amelia was going to be seeing the bakery for the first time Sunday night.

But he hadn't seen Maddie. And as much as he'd expected that to come as a relief, by the time he'd loaded up his truck and pulled into the driveway of his house, he realized that the only thing he felt was disappointment.

The check that had quietly arrived in his mailbox on Friday afternoon, not posted, but rather placed, sat with the stack of envelopes and bills.

Cole looked away, focused on pulling out four slices of fresh bread—two for each of them—and setting them in the toaster.

He waited, wondering if his mother would say something now. Or if she'd eat her toast and then they'd get on with the day. If she'd stopped pushing him onto Maddie Conway.

If she'd given up.

His stomach knotted as he stared into the red coils of the toaster, knowing that he didn't even want toast this morning. He didn't want to go about his day like he usually did and always had.

He wanted more.

Abruptly, he stopped the toaster and turned to his mother. "I was thinking I might treat you to breakfast at Buttercream Bakery," he said.

There. It was out. Decision made. And even though his heart was pounding at the implication of this simple invitation, he felt more alive than he had in years. And happier, too.

And from the broad smile that reached all the way up to his mother's shining eyes, it was clear that the same could be said for her.

*

It seemed that half of Maddie's concerns about the bakery vanished in the first hour of business, and she was too busy tending to customers, overseeing her new employee, and checking on her baked goods in the kitchen to even think about the other half.

Granted, most of her first customers were family members and friends, but then, this was Blue Harbor. Practically everyone in town was a friend of some sort, or at least, an acquaintance. Still, it warmed her heart to see everyone come out to support her, and it made her even more pleased to see the expression on their faces when they studied her display case, which was just bursting with fall favorites like cranberry scones and apple turnovers and, of course, her ever-popular cinnamon rolls. Amelia had already sent over three people this morning in search of their daily fix.

Amy was in the kitchen while Maddie tended to the

customers. It wouldn't always be this way, but Maddie had arrived before dawn to get everything prepped and ready and she wanted to be sure to greet every customer on her big day. Now, as the first rush dwindled, she took stock of what remained in the case, deciding that she should probably pop another sheet pan of the apple cinnamon coffee cake into the oven. It was turning out to be one of her top sellers.

She checked the door one more time, and then hurried to the kitchen, where Amy was drizzling cream cheese frosting over the cinnamon rolls. She was rosy-cheeked and humming. Maddie couldn't help but smile. They'd worked together for a good portion of the weekend getting ready for this day, and she was nearly as grateful for the help as she was the company.

Being alone didn't suit her any more than working alone did, she'd come to realize. It was so much more satisfying to share an experience.

Amy looked up. "Cinnamon rolls are ready."

"Great! Why don't you bring those out and cover the counter while I make another coffee cake?"

Amy didn't need further direction. She grabbed an oven mitt, lifted the pan, and scooted back into the storefront. The sweet smell that wafted behind her was one that Maddie never tired of, and she knew people in Blue Harbor didn't either. Those cinnamon rolls were her staple at Firefly Café and they had earned her a stamp of approval in this town.

Maddie went to work quickly with a fresh mixing bowl, measuring the ingredients without needing to consult her recipe book. She looked down at her mother's apron as she worked, feeling her heart fill with fond memories, and said a silent thank you to the woman who had really been the one to make this all possible.

Because she couldn't have done it on her own.

She had just set the timer when there was a knock on the swing door.

Immediately, Maddie tensed. Yes, she was in a much better place with Candy, but that didn't mean she needed the woman stopping by mere hours into her first day.

"Come in," she said warily, hoping that it might be her father instead. Her sisters and cousins would be busy at their own businesses today, after all.

She braced herself for Candy's energy and enthusiasm, only it wasn't Candy at all. It was Cole.

Her heart began a slow and steady drum. "Cole." She let the word hang there. Didn't know what else to say, really. Had he not received his check? Had Candy deliberately not dropped it off to prompt this moment?

But no, she knew now that Candy had no part of this. That Candy had said to let him be. Let him search his soul a bit.

Now, with a fresh surge of hope that she almost didn't dare to feel, Maddie wondered if Candy had been right.

Again.

Cole shoved his hands into the front pockets of his jeans, giving her a little grin. "I realized that I never did get to try one of those cinnamon rolls that Candy was telling me about."

Maddie swallowed hard. She stood by the center island, in the kitchen that he had built. The kitchen that felt like it was just as much his as it was hers.

"I just made a fresh batch. If you go out to the counter now, you can probably still get one."

He nodded slowly but showed no intention of moving. "The thing is that walking out to that counter means walking away from you again. And…I don't want to do that."

She blinked at him. Waited. Wanted to believe that he meant what he was saying. That he wanted what she did. That he believed that there could be a future in this little town, despite the difficulty of the past.

He took a step toward her. She felt herself stiffen.

"I'm not as tough as I look, Cole," she said. "I put up walls, too. I don't want to feel hurt again either."

He didn't argue with her. "These past few weeks were some of the best days that I've ever had in this town. Maybe it was because I finally let those walls come down. Or maybe it was because of you."

"Because of me?" She'd only given him a job, really, and not by choice. "I was just being myself, Cole. I wasn't trying to push you or change your mind."

"But you did," he said, giving her a slow grin. He reached out, took her hand. His palm was warm, big, and she wanted to snatch her hand back as much she never wanted him to let it go.

"You need to do what's best for you. I know what it's like, to lose someone you love."

"I thought I did, too, until I started thinking about how it would feel to lose you." He met her eyes, and for a moment, her breath caught. "I want to stay, Maddie. I want to start over. I want to let people in. I don't want to hide anymore. And I guess I'm putting it all out there. Seeing what you'll say."

She searched his eyes, so deep and intense, the same eyes that had been unreadable once, that now seemed to bore straight through to her heart.

"I think I should almost be mad at you, but I can't," she said, fighting off a smile that stretched across her face, matching the one he now wore.

"Because—"

"Because now I have to admit that Candy was right," Maddie said, laughing. She reached out and took his other hand. He squeezed it gently, showing no signs of letting go as he leaned down and kissed her slowly. And sweetly.

ABOUT THE AUTHOR

Olivia Miles is a *USA Today* bestselling author of feel-good women's fiction with a romantic twist. She has frequently been ranked as an Amazon Top 100 author, and her books have appeared on several bestseller lists, including Amazon charts, BookScan, and USA Today. Treasured by readers across the globe, Olivia's heartwarming stories have been translated into German, French, and Hungarian, with editions in Australia in the United Kingdom.

Olivia lives on the shore of Lake Michigan with her family.

Visit www.OliviaMilesBooks.com for more.

Made in United States
Troutdale, OR
06/28/2023

10869982R00130